Murder on BROADWAY

Sondra Luger

Gotham Books
30 N Gould St.
Ste. 20820, Sheridan, WY 82801
https://gothambooksinc.com/
Phone: 1 (307) 464-7800

Published by Gotham Books (February 6, 2023)

ISBN: 979-8-88775-119-1 (h)
ISBN: 978-1-956349-40-5 (sc)
ISBN: 978-1-956349-41-2 (e)

Other books by the Author

Rich, Never Married, Rich
Back from Bora Bora
Drop Me Off in Harlem

With appreciation for excerpts from Lilly Dache's autobiography,
TALKING THROUGH MY HATS, ed.
Dorothy Roe Lewis, Coward McCann, Inc., 1946

Chapter One

"She won't divorce him." Tenisha Jones eyed the apple in her hands before taking a bite.

"That's not what she said," responded her friend and fellow fashion model Lily Ann Chasen. "She told Molly she wouldn't divorce him unless he found her a husband as wonderful as he is."

"Same thing. No man thinks he's less than the best."

"Ted thinks I'm too good for him," mused Lily, "and Donald think you're a goddess."

"Ted does fall all over himself for you, and Donald does keep raising my pedestal, but men like Roland Trane, obscenely wealthy, tall, handsome, respected businessman and philanthropists, men like him have cloud-high opinions of themselves."

Lee Chasen rested the fork in the salad and folded the newspaper, turning it toward her friend. "Adoration doesn't get any deeper than that."

Tenisha Jones looked at the picture of the two Trane socialites entering the theater for an opening night. "She is a good actress, they say."

"That adoration looks real to me."

"A very good actress. That's something you don't forget to be, even offstage, if necessary, and especially as the years go by, when you really need to remember."

"Why so cynical, Ten?"

Tenisha Jones took another bite of the apple. "I've been reading too much. Who's our good mayor Jimmy Walker been seen with lately? Two beds, maybe, two bedrooms, maybe, but two apartments?"

"Jimmy Walker's wife is hardly poor financially, and so the arrangement."

"An arrangement that can kill a woman in more ways than financial. At least the public doesn't know yet about poor Mrs. Trane. She's been spared that for a while longer." Tenisha placed the remnant of her apple in the coffee saucer. "Molly has finished shortening the hem on Mildred Trane's new taffeta dress, so we won't get more news before the newspapers do. Pitiful world. Glamour doesn't have to be like that."

"You and I will keep it aloft, Ten. When does Coulet need you in Paris to model his fall collection?"

"August. I'm thrilled that Bernie is also using me for his Coulet adaptations, and that Negro designers are so interested in advertising my legs, hands and head. Now I've got to keep all of me in shape, like you!"

"Margaret keeps complaining about your replacement."

"Well, she's not getting me back, unless she wants me to model with her accounting books." Lily laughed.

"She might at that."

The door of the lounge flew open, and Molly, wide-eyed, breathless, and holding the sides of the door for support, shouted at them, "She's been arrested for trying to kill her husband! She's at the police station!"

Lily and Tenisha rushed to her side. "Calm down, calm down," said Lily, as they ushered her toward the sofa. "What's happened? Speak slowly."

Molly took a deep breath. "Roland Trane was in the library getting a book from a high shelf when someone pushed the ladder out from under him. Mrs. Trane was the only one in the house, so she's at the police station for questioning."

"Being brought in for questioning is not the same as being arrested for attempted murder," said Lily. "How badly hurt was Mr. Trane?"

"Oh, he wasn't hurt at all. He put his feet on the shelves beneath and lowered himself to the floor."

"Molly, Molly!" The voice of an agitated Bernard Singer reverberated through the halls of Bernard Singer Couture before the couturier himself burst into the lounge. "Didn't I tell you to be quiet, didn't I tell you not to upset the girls? We don't need another Lizette Frere debacle at this House!"

"No one's been murdered here," said Molly in defense, "and Mrs. Trane is just a client." She was whimpering now.

"Out! Back to work! Just a client. One of our best, one who's looked up to for her character, her talent, her clothes. Our clothes! My clothes! Girls, this goes no further—" There was a hubbub in the hall. "Too late! Lee, Tenisha, see if you can bring the girls to their senses. Why is it so hard to get some sanity in this house? Oh, by the way, Lee, Mrs. Trane wants to see you at the police station with pins, tape measure, scissors, whatever Molly uses. Don't ask me why. I don't question Mildred Trane. Not a word to anyone, not a word! Oh, lord, oh, lord!" And the bushy-haired designer left the lounge.

Chapter Two

"Y ou!"

"Good afternoon, Inspector."

"I'm sorry, Mrs. Trane. If Miss Chasen thinks this is a police case she can stick her nose into, she's mistaken."

"I'm sure she thinks nothing of the sort, Inspector Kirk."

Apparently no one was going to address Lily directly. "Mrs. Trane was late for her fitting, so here I am, as per instructions from my boss, to do the same for her in the comfort of her home, arrival to same via company van, since her chauffeur will not return from the barber for several hours."

"Neat. How much hair does the man have?" growled Kirk.

Mrs.Trane stood and shook Inspector Kirk's hand. "May I leave now?"

"Of course, of course," he said, his gun clattering to the floor. He quickly retrieved it. "A woman of your stature ... but you understand why I had to see you."

"I do, indeed. Goodbye."

The inspector rubbed his chin as they departed. "A model doing alterations? She's up to something, but there is nothing to be up to. Accidents happen. Hmm."

Lily put the Ford van into drive and pulled away from the curb.

"I'm afraid the inspector's still smarting from the publicity you and your friend got from solving the Lizette Frere murder last year. You want to know why I asked for you and pins and tape measure when Molly's already fitted me? I'll tell you. I admire the way you handled that case, and I need a woman to help me too, before I become another Lizette Frere — respected, feared and dead!"

Lily shot a quick glance at Mildred Trane before exiting the highway and entering the private road that led to the Trane mansion.

"What the inspector doesn't know is that I was nearly pushed down the stairs soon after Roland yelled for me from the library. Naturally, he would think that it was me. Who else was in the house? I was pushed, I know it, pushed, but I grabbed hold of the banister to break the fall. I twisted my ankle and tore my dress, as you will see. Row may have kicked the ladder to the side, himself, it wouldn't be the first time. He can be absent-minded when he's absorbed in something. I was in a hurry to get down the stairs to him when I felt a pressure in my back. The house isn't haunted, and I'm not crazy."

Lily Ann Chasen and Mildred Trane scrunched sand from the driveway to the house, an imposing nineteenth century English mansion, which Trane's father had thought suitable for his home. The staff, given time off after a weekend of special activity, were now in evidence for afternoon tea in the library. Mrs. Trane smiled graciously at them and did not speak until they had left the room.

"You are aware Row wants to divorce me." Lily nodded. "I've been dreading this for years. He needs me, and I guess I need him. I've ignored his flirtations—maybe they were more, I didn't want to know—because I know he needs my strength, my support to be what he wants to be, respected as a man of talent and power."

"But I thought he was. His cosmetics are constantly winning accolades and awards."

"Insiders know better. His true business successes have been in selecting a staff at Trane & Co. that can do what he can't. He gets the admiration, and they're willing to settle for outsized salaries and fantastic recommendations should they decide to leave. Only one has. Roland's two previous wives were showgirls, beautiful, appealing, but not much in the brains department, except how to catch a husband. Then I came along, a serious actress, admired, thought by many to be attractive, with theater glitz and substance. Row could bask in reflected glory, but that can only last so long. The day comes when you realize it isn't enough, when you want to be the object of admiration yourself. Row wanted to be an actor. Did you know that? When that didn't work out, he became a backer of Broadway plays, but he wants to be respected for his talent, not his money."

"And what is his talent?"

"Getting along with people, being a sweet man with a lovely temperament and a sunny personality, being kind and considerate. But he wants to be respected for what he does not who he is. I can't give him a lifetime of that. No one can. So it's back to the chorus line for him, where compared to Suzie Sweet, he's a person of substance who doesn't have to weigh what he considers his deficits against what he perceives as my attributes. He can move on to wife number four. But I don't want to lose him."

"But your request—"

"That he provide me with another him? He thinks it's possible. He's compiling a list of prospects for me to consider and will provide excuses for them to meet with me individually. They'll be wealthy and like Row, so he thinks. He has no idea what he's like!"

"Clever, this idea of yours."

"Not mine. It's the premise of a play that opened last month, *The Behavior of Mrs. Crane*. Trane, Crane, I liked the sound of it and the premise. Row thought it quite clever of me too. Perhaps I was too clever. The play closed last week."

"What do you want me to do for you?"

"Apart from fixing the hem I tore, I'd like you to find out who wants to kill me. Suzie Sweet would be the obvious suspect, if she hadn't been in a matinee performance. I checked; she was there. With me gone, there's no impediment to making Miss Sweet wife number four, but if neither she nor Row were in a position to push me, who was? Who would want to?"

"Who brought the library incident to the attention of the police?"

"My attorney, William Branten. When Row exited the library, Branten was at the front door, and Row, with his theatrical instincts and still reeling from the ladder scare, told him the story. William thought the incident warranted a call to the police. A precaution, he said. The city is full of nuts."

"Perhaps both of you were the objects of some crazy burglar."

"All windows and doors were closed and locked. Nothing was taken. Maybe Row wasn't absent-minded this time. Maybe we're both in danger."

"Danger sounds like something outside a model's sphere. With Lizette Frere, Tenisha and I were in the right place at the right time, pursuing justice for a friend, a model we'd worked with daily."

"I'm in your sphere. I'm an excellent Singer Couture client who wears his clothes both on and off the stage. My recommendations have brought tens of thousands of dollars of business to the firm, and I plan to do much more."

Then hire Bernard Singer to take your case, thought Lily. I'm just a model there. But she said, "I don't think I can do this case, if that's what it is, justice. I think professional help would serve you better. And between modeling jobs and singing preparation, I have no time –"

"Ah, yes. You want to be an opera singer, but lessons from a titan of operatic singing like Wilhelm Strauss—"

"Oh, I could never afford someone of his caliber—"

"But I can, and I know him well. He rarely takes on new students, but he owes me a lot. Well, what do you say?"

"I'll fix your hem, while I'm here, but that's all. My talents don't run in the direction you would like."

Mildred Trane pursed her lips and offered her hem.

Chapter Three

The applause rang through the Metropolitan Opera House. Lily, her eyes glowing, turned to Ted. "Thank you, darling. I do so love *La Rondine*! Wasn't Lucrezia Bori magnificent?"

"Not as magnificent as you'll be."

Lily laughed. "You're fan club member number one."

They slowly followed the crowd into the lobby, where clusters of people were chatting, eating pastry and drinking sodas. Ted cupped his mouth and ordered champagne and reached over a lady's head to accept it.

"I haven't been here since I treated myself when I came to New York three years ago. We can thank Bori and Gigli for this mob scene."

"Someday you'll be making your debut here. If you want Wilhem Strauss as a vocal coach, I can help you. You don't need the likes of Mildred Trane to blackmail you into it. I've been putting aside extra cash for our honeymoon, but you come first. We don't have to get married right away."

"Did I say we were getting married at all? Talk about blackmail!" Lily squeezed Ted's hand and smiled up into his anxious face. "Oh, look, there's the desperate woman herself." A cluster of people parted, revealing Mildred and Roland Trane, dressed to the nines, arm in arm, heading back to their seats. "It's an opening night, so it's not odd that she and I are here at the same time, is it? I only told Ten and—Bernie! Still, it can only be a coincidence. She hasn't approached us."

But Mildred Trane had turned abruptly, turning with her the two men with whose hands hers were entwined. Her face registered pleasure as she and her captive males bore down on Lily and Ted.

"What a delightful surprise," she enthused. "Roland, Wilhelm, I'd like you to meet my favorite model at my favorite couturier. She's Lily Ann Chasen, and with her is Ted Martin, vice president at Martin Fabrics. Young people, meet my husband Roland and one of the greatest vocal teachers of all time, Wilhelm Strauss. You know, Wilhelm, Lily has an amazing soprano voice that only needs the touch of a teaching master to rise to the standards of the Metropolitan Opera."

"I always pray to discover singers with such talent, but my prayers have only intermittently been answered."

"This may be one of those intermittent moments," suggested Mildred Trane.

"Perhaps. I have no objection to listening to the young lady, but, Miss Chasen, I can guarantee nothing, you understand, as much as I respect the opinions of Mrs. Trane." He bowed slightly toward her, hampered somewhat by the arm with which she firmly held his.

Lily blushed. "You are most kind. Mrs. Trane is most kind."

The bell indicating that the next act would begin in a few minutes enabled Lily to cut the conversation short with what she hoped looked like a grateful smile, as she hurried off with Ted to their seats. The young couple reached them as the lights dimmed.

"Desperation can always recognize an amazing voice she's never heard," said Lily, as the curtain rose on Act II.

Chapter Four

"Lily, so glad you're early. You have the perfect head for my Cockeyed Twist hat. At last, I can see what it looks like on the right head." The milliner's face registered delight.

"This doesn't sound flattering, Miss Daché."

"Oh, it is, it is. Your head is an extension of your face. So versatile. It can say so many things, sometimes all at once."

"Oh, dear! What is it saying now?"

"That you are braced for whatever that Trane woman throws at you."

"Miss Daché! You speaking ill of a client?" "Never! She goes to Sally Victor."

"Just what have you heard?"

"Turn around, I want to start wrapping." Lilly Daché took three strands of fabric in her left hand—one silk, one velvet, one chiffon—and started swirling them every which way around Lily's head, which she held firmly in her right hand. "Oh, your head is blooming! How exciting you look!" She moved Lily to the floor-length mirror. She had bent points of silk and velvet into loops dancing on Lily's head. "Charmante!" Miss Daché pulled wisps of hair over Lily's forehead and swirled curls toward her face in front of either ear. "Schiaparelli would have kept and reinforced the points. Quelle catastrophe!"

"Please tell me what you've heard, Miss Daché."

"That a hat like this will meet the test for Sally Victor's client, so I allow it, even though the hat will not be for others to see for another six weeks. Pierre! Shoot her this way." Lily's right profile was photographed. "Now this way." Her left profile got the same treatment. "Now this." Lily's face and hat were immortalized from the front. "Merveilleux."

Lilly Daché placed photographs of assorted backgrounds behind Lily's head — exotic views, park views, theater views. "So versatile, the hat, the head. Ah, Lily, you only miss perfection by one '1'. C'est la vie. You will do well tomorrow."

"Am I going somewhere tomorrow?"

"If you wish. That is for you to decide."

"It sounds like others have decided it for me."

Lilly Daché shrugged. "It is not for me to gossip."

"Isn't it?"

"Certainement pas!" Her voice rang with authority. "Go, go! Tell me how he liked the hat," and she hastily left the dressing room, meekly followed by the photographer.

"He?" Lily Ann Chasen stared into one of the elegant mirrors. Would Miss Daché say the same if she were a blonde? A mischievous glint shone in Lily's eyes. Someday she would find out.

"You're early! Well, you're here. Coffee? Tea?" They were alone in the Morning Room.

Not even a good rote speech for an actress, thought Lily. "No, thank you."

"Then we'll have to wait."

"For what?"

"For when you are ready for coffee or tea."

"Mrs. Trane, why did you ask Bernard Singer to send me here?"

"You are a model who wears cloche hats well. I am an actress who does not. However, I am about to embark on a new look, with close-cut hair that is a departure from my waves and curls. Roland and I will be attending a gala, and I need a professional model to look over my wardrobe, very Bernard Singer, you understand, and decide which of my gowns would look best with my new look. Nice hat, by the way. Lilly Daché?"

"Yes, thank you. You might consider adding this daring look to your outfit."

"Perhaps. Please come with me."

Up the hall's center staircase they went, as Lily mused that the Daché exuberance, authority and style would be too much competition for the queen of the theater. Lily was led to a Louis XV bedroom. She wondered if the double beds were part of the Trane problem. Her hostess called her attention to the wardrobe, which she now swung open with a flourish. She pulled out the skirts of some glittering ball gowns.

"We're the same size, so try them on and see what looks best on you."

Lily recalled a Daché admonition: "Your personality and character dictate how you will look in a garment, whether you can carry it off. Your appearance and your measurements pale before them."

"May I consider other gowns?"

"Other designers." Mrs. Trane waved them away.

"May I consider them anyway?"

"Bernard will be upset if you select someone else's work."

"Mr. Singer will not be wearing the gown. It has to look right on you. What image are you trying to convey?"

"Charming, but daring; sweet, but strong; caring, trusting, proud, but acceptably so."

"And how do you plan to get the two heads you'll need through the neck of the gown?"

Mildred Trane laughed. "We all have opposing aspects to our personality."

"Are these opposing aspects part of yours?"

"They can be."

"You want your husband to see you in a new, exciting light, and the dress is to assist you."

"Exactly. Please get started." She left the room before Lily could question further.

Lily sighed. "A dress can never make the woman. It's the woman who makes the dress. She's a good actress, Tenisha said, a very good actress, but is that enough? We'll see," thought Lily, as she took a Schiaparelli off the hanger. Schiaparelli and daring were practically synonymous. Mrs. Trane in her new hairdo would have to supply the other attributes. "I'm not a magician," thought Lily, "but maybe

Mildred Trane is." And she pulled the Schiaparelli with wings over her bodice and looked thoughtfully in the boudoir's floor-length mirror.

Mildred Trane was en route to the front door, as was Roderick, the butler. At her nod, he strode off.

"Willie, darling, I knew I could count on you. Thanks so much."

"Old friends need no thanks. Where's the cosmetics king?"

"You know he's not home yet." She took him by the hand, led him into the Morning Room and sat him by her side. "You've heard, of course."

"Words in the wind, my dear. I give them no credence without your approval."

"Roland's latest escapade is serious."

"Escapades are never serious, Mildred."

"They can lead to something serious. They can lead to divorce. I don't want to be his third failure unless there's another husband that would at least make it worthwhile for me."

"Marriage worthwhile? It sounds like a business agreement, and that doesn't sound like you."

"What kind of man do you think would make me happy, Willie?"

"I've hinted narrowly for years someone who would be ideal. Someone artistic and caring, strong, not needy, who adores his wife, supports her independence and talent. Someone like me. In fact—me exactly! Of course, there is the little matter of reciprocation, which as I've told you for years, you've been lavishing on the wrong man."

"If I did reciprocate, if I dared to reciprocate with someone as wonderful as you, would you marry me?"

Willie sputtered up the lemonade Roderick had left on the Morning Room table, coughing uncontrollably for a minute before he recovered. "You mean you *would* marry me?"

"I'm not saying I would, only that should I consider it, would I be wasting my time?"

"Certainly not! Oh, dear Mildred, I can't believe the possibility exists! I've never believed the possibility existed. This is more than I've ever hoped for!"

Roderick reappeared. "Telephone call, Mrs. Trane."

"Excuse me for a moment, Willie."

"Of course, my dear, of course." Willie pushed the lemonade aside. "Lord, lord," he muttered. "Such a dear friend. Never dreamed of this."

"Are you pushing that drink aside because you don't want it, or because you're offering it to me?"

It was Lily, a vision in a wing-spread collar and pinched waist of a chiffon floral print in yellow and red.

"For you, definitely for you! And you are —?"

"Lily Ann Chasen, a model at Bernard Singer Couture. Would you like to see Mrs. Trane in this dress?"

"Why, are you giving it away?"

Lily laughed. "It's not mine to give. Well, would you?"

"Are you a dress burglar? I'd much rather hear you're a dress burglar than a model."

"Sorry."

"Well, since you've asked, I'd say that pointed arch collar would be very Mrs. Trane, but it's more exciting on you."

"Why is that?"

"Because the rest of you is so different. A very inviting contrast, very. And that hat, yes, very exciting." He looked Lily over from head to toe with beaming approval.

"And my hair?"

"Your hair? What the dickens has your hair got to do with it?"

"Indeed. So, Mr.—"

"Willie Simpson. My friends call me Willie."

"But I'm not one of your friends."

"Yet, Lily Ann Chasen. But you will be."

"What makes you so sure?"

"I've a sixth sense about women who are not in their element, but are anxious to get in. You're more than a model, and that cheeky introduction that you threw at me indicates you want me to be your friend."

"Very Sherlock of you." He looked at her for a more significant response. "I'm an opera singer, too, in training."

"With whom?"

"No one at the moment. Voice lessons require payment. However, with modeling savings behind me, I'm now on the verge of acquiring one."

"On the verge, are you? I'm glad to hear it. It's time opera singers offered visual as well as vocal appeal, otherwise I might as well stay home and listen to them on the radio. I would, too, if the opera house were not the 'in' social place to be for elegant people."

Lily laughed. "So you consider yourself elegant?"

"Of course. Mildred Trane isn't the only one who can act. I just do my acting on a different stage, the stage of upper-class life. It's amusing, gratifying, and passes the time most agreeably."

"Have you an occupation, or do you nurse an obscenely large income your parents left you?"

"Oh, I like you! Actually, I do both. As an only child, I inherited my parents' building construction fortune. I can live as I please, and it pleases me to be a publisher of books about buildings, fascinating objects that unmask human nature as few other objects do. Because of my heritage, I'm deemed an expert on houses, so I'm able to enjoy the pleasure of producing books on the subject and the more intriguing pleasure of extricating human foibles and fancies from the builders and building occupants, all the while relaxing in the social nonsense my position entitles me to. I lead a very well-rounded life."

"Congratulations. Do you think I'll take you on as a friend to get help in forwarding my career?"

"Take me on. That's interesting. You're a bold little thing, but apparently you have no interest in doing the expected. Very stimulating."

"I'm sure the multi-faceted Mrs. Trane is more stimulating."

Willie drew back a bit on the sofa. "What are you doing here, anyway?"

"I'm here in my capacity as a model. Mrs. Trane may appear in public in the very ensemble you behold."

He nodded, smiling. "She'll be able to carry it off. She's a very good actress."

They both had the prescience to look up. In the doorway stood Mildred Trane.

Chapter Five

"Always have a garden, says my mother."
Tenisha sat with Lily on green plastic chairs on the garden strip bordering the Harlem brownstone that was home.

The garden was sprouting some early spring hair, and some leaves had taken up residence on the lone, live tree. A six-foot fence blocked out the row of houses across the street. It sported sturdy painted tree trunks with full heads of green leaves.

"My retired neighbors are busy preparing dinner and listening to the radio. We've got the perfect antidote to Singer Couture mayhem." Tenisha pulled her sweater closer against the slight early evening chill.

"This is wonderful," Lily agreed. "Mr. Foster's garden on the floor below me is one reason I took my apartment. I can look at it, even if I can't visit it without invitation. The old darling is always willing to accommodate me, but he is entitled to his privacy."

"My landlady likes things to get full use, at her idea of the appropriate time. All tenants have gotten calls about having their lights on before sundown. Lee, I wanted to talk to you away from Bernie and the girls. I've had an offer from Elsa Schiaparelli to model for her House, and I don't know what to do."

"Wow! Schiap! You'll make headlines with anything you do for her."

"I don't know if I want to make headlines. Donald will be teaching history next year. A low-key assignment with Coulet might suit his lifestyle better."

"You're not married to him yet. A fling with Schiap's clothes will get the adventuress out of your system."

"You know there's not an ounce of the adventuress in my system."

"A little taste of it won't hurt. Then you can tell your kids that once you walked on the wild side."

"But with Coulet I can tell them I was 'in' at the beginning of an exciting new designer."

"To kids, 'in at the beginning' makes you look old."

"You're no help, Lee."

"All right. Why can't you model for both houses? Designers compete, sure, but there's no intrinsic competition here. One is new and far in, and one is established and far out; one is French and the other Italian."

"Do you think they would go for such an arrangement?"

"Probably not. Either way, you'd be out of the country a lot. Too long a trip for dinner and dancing with Donald. With Coulet, at least, it's part time in Paris. You'll be modeling his clothes adaptations for the American market here in New York, with Bernie. What does Donald say?"

"I haven't told him yet. First a Negro model has a devil of a time getting any job, and then she gets one too many."

"Not any Negro model. *You*, my talented friend."

"Thanks, Lee. I've got two weeks to decide, but I don't want anyone at Singer to know until I do."

"If it's a 'yes,' to Schiap, your stock soars everywhere, if it's a 'no,' your stock soars with Coulet and Singer."

"And Donald. By the way, I got a call from Coulet about Suzie Sweet. She's a new client, and he'd like to know something about her—style, color preferences, the works. He thinks her competition may have dropped some comments about her during one of her visits to Singer. As far as I know, Mildred has not. Thank goodness. I don't want anything to do with a woman-eat-woman fight."

"I'm already in it." Lily touched a rosebud on one of the bushes. "I love roses."

"Well, Miss Conservative-Lover-of-Roses, what have you got yourself into now?"

"Mildred Trane wants to look like me, at least for an opening night theater party she'll be attending with Roland. She used my hairstyle as an excuse; she's going to imitate it. She's trying to excite Roland on the one hand and at least one old beau on the other. She was testing his reaction to the clothes and to me when I went to her home. He 'accidentally' showed up. She was a touch worried when I arrived early and was afraid I'd be gone before he appeared. She thought she was fooling me. I think that acting in real life is harder than on the stage!"

"This is hilarious. She wants to look like a flapper, and Suzie Sweet wants to look more respectable! So, you did what she wanted, as per Bernie's request."

"Not completely. She wants me to find out who wants to kill her. When Roland had the ladder incident and shouted for her, someone tried to push her down the stairs, or so she thinks."

"If so, it was Suzie Sweet. Case closed."

"No, she was in a matinee performance at the time."

"I don't want to hear any more about this. I won't speak tales to Coulet, should any come my way, and you're not getting involved in something that could lead to lawsuits and Inspector Kirk's fury."

"You're right, of course, Ten. But why would a level-headed woman feel she's being pushed down the stairs in an empty house?"

Chapter Six

"Are you sure you want my opinion, Mildred? I put together bridges and buildings, not clothing ensembles." Robert Blair looked decidedly uncomfortable.

Mildred Trane sipped the red wine on the lone table facing the runway in Bernard Singer's showroom. "Oh, yes, your opinion will be invaluable to me. I want clothes that are practical, but feminine, and who more practical than an engineer?" She gave a nod toward the stage wings, and the showing began. Sally, Margo and Lily would parade twenty ensembles, with Lily displaying a disproportionate ten of the twenty.

"Good lord!" This for an irregular hem on a dress modeled by Lily.

"Louiseboulanger started the craze for it last year," explained Mildred.

"Who?"

The polka-dot velvet dress with a mandarin collar caused Blair to take off his eyeglasses and wipe them. "Unsettling design," he intoned, "and a heavy look." To a satin ball gown, "Shimmers, and gives coverage. Good."

In all, Robert approved three conservative pieces of apparel, two of them floral. Tenisha watched from the wings, shaking her head. She joined Lily in the dressing room after the presentation.

"His choices would be embarrassing at any high-toned social affair."

"The fashion rabble be damned," said Lily. "He likes what he likes."

"You modeled the most attractive avant garde pieces, and he didn't choose one. He didn't look at you with any kind or degree of appreciation."

"No, it was hard to miss the thrilled expression on Mrs. Trane's face. I modeled enough clothes to assure her that neither the clothes nor I posed a threat. She wants marital security. She's likely to get it with her engineer, not financial, though."

"Her pre-marital contract assures her of one-third of Roland's fortune in a divorce."

"True, Ten, and she won't need more, but she'd get two-thirds if he dies, which is possible if he tries to keep up with Suzie Sweet."

"I hope she's got a tight contract if she marries someone middle class, like Robert."

"She probably has. Attorney Branten has proven his worth in this regard with plenty of women. But beyond money, Robert Blair seems a bit stiff compared to Willie Simpson, who actually proposed marriage to her multiple times. Of course, he was pretty safe in his anticipation of refusal. He liked the Daché hat, though; that speaks well for him. I don't know why Robert looked so horrified when he saw it. It has a bridge-spanning quality to it."

"Maybe he doesn't want his wife to remind him of his work. There may be hope for him yet, Lee." The girls had just entered the lounge for a brief sit-down before leaving for the day when Bernard Singer blasted into the room.

"Girls, you've got to help me keep Mildred Trane."

"Oh, she told you about the Schiaparelli?"

"What Schiaparelli? Someone is trying to take her away from me. She's on the sofa in my office with that mathematician fanning her."

"He's not a mathemat—"

"I've called a doctor. The social season is in full swing, and Mildred Trane may be out of commission with a broken leg. Some idiot, no, some enemy left a banana skin right outside our door, and she fell!"

"She can still appear in public," said Tenisha.

"How, with a cane, a crutch, in a wheelchair? How would my clothes look in those settings! Singer clothes for invalids is not the image I wish to convey!"

"A dependent woman may not be a bad image for her," mused Lily. "But it may merely be a slight strain," she quickly added, as Singer seemed on the verge of apoplexy.

Bernard Singer took a deep breath, exhaled, and stated with feigned calm, "Let's hope so. She did make light of it, said it was like a stupid comedy act she'd seen recently with Roland, then blushed and waved the thought away."

"Could she be trying to blame Roland?" suggested Tenisha.

"Why would Roland hate me? What have I ever done to him?"

Lily put her right hand to her face. Did Bernie really think that anything that happened to a client had something to do with him, that clients' lives revolved around Bernard Singer Couture? She looked intently at his face. Yes, she thought, I guess he does.

"Roland's too obvious a culprit," said Tenisha.

"Obvious or not, I want you both to find out who injured our client. I'd call the police, but it happened right outside our door. The publicity—"

"Why us?"

"Because, Lee, she specifically asked for you and Tenisha. She said you've done it before, you can do it again."

"Does she see a similarity between the murder of Lizette Frere and the danger she thinks she's in?"

"I don't know what she sees. I only know that when my best client, who has thousands of admirers hanging on her every word and calling in droves for her every outfit, says she wants two of my models to help her, I don't refuse!"

"Ten and I will check our schedules, but I know that next week I have an appointment with Lilly Daché to—"

"Lilly Daché be hanged! I'll pay you double, triple what she'll give you!"

"It's not the money—" The deadly look on Singer's face silenced her. Her job with Singer was close to full time. "How do you propose we proceed?"

"How, Lee, how? Do I have to tell you everything?" And he stormed out.

Lily turned to her friend. "Do banana skins hold fingerprints?"

Tenisha shrugged.

Chapter Seven

"You have your wish."

Mildred Trane, in a stunning two-piece Singer dress of orange and black, with the sweater open for a deceptively casual look, was not surprised.

"Mr. Singer has given me and Tenisha one week in which to resolve, rectify and satisfy both your concerns and his."

"Wonderful! In five days, we move from an attic to actual theater rehearsals for my next play. I'll be able to concentrate fully on the script with this matter behind me. The play has been running unsuccessfully for years, but Roland has revised it, and we expect a smash hit."

"Running for—not *The Ladder*!"

"Yes, indeed! It's about to experience a resurrection!"

"But why *The Ladder*?"

"The multiple roles are a challenge, and I like the theme. Now, how do you plan to accomplish our goal in one week?"

"Before I determine that, I need to know what unexpected events have befallen you of late, and with what frequency."

"Apart from my banana fiasco — I'm sure you recognized it for what it was; I know how to fall onstage — there was one thing in the past week. As I was walking down the street last Monday, a green diamond bracelet on a mannequin at Saks caught my eye. I stopped at the window for a closer look. It looked exactly like one Roland had custom-made for me for our anniversary."

"When did Suzie Sweet come into your lives?"

Mildred Trane looked surprised. "At about that time. When I returned home, I looked in my jewelry box, and my bracelet was gone.

I returned immediately, oh, maybe two hours later, to Saks, but the bracelet on the mannequin had been replaced by a green enamel one. I hurried home to my jewelry box, and my bracelet had returned."

"Do any of the characters you will be playing wear green jewelry?"

"I know what you're thinking but—"

"Do they?"

"Roland did devise a green scene, with various shades of green on walls, drapery, upholstery, and yes, jewelry on my person, but nothing like this. And jealousy is prominent in the play, you know, so it's very effective. But the play was the furthest thing from my mind when I looked at the Saks window. I was thinking of the dinner I asked Marta to prepare for some guests Thursday night."

"Will Roland be there?"

"Of course, he'll be there. It's essential that he be there. We'll be discussing final changes to the revised play with Murdock Pemberton. He wrote the last eighteen versions of the play, yes, eighteen. There's no point in your not knowing, it will be in all the newspapers soon. Roland has a small part in the new production, and he funded the new scenery, costumes and technology that add an important supernatural element that connects the episodes that span the centuries. If you've seen *The Ladder,* you can imagine what changes these shots of adrenaline can make in the play."

"I saw the play and found it memorable." Lily didn't add that seeing it with Ted Martin so angered the senior Martin that he fired her. Not only was Ted helping her with her office work at Martin Fabrics, he was dating her as well. Outrageous! Lily was replaced by a forty-five-year-old spinster who dressed as if she were sixty. Hardly suitable at the House of an acclaimed fabric designer, but oh, well.

"What did you find memorable about it?"

"I thought it well-scripted and well-acted, but it wasn't emotionally exciting or intellectually stimulating. Maybe if the episodes had been longer and more conclusive, it might have been. I liked the theme, though, that what you do in one lifetime determines what becomes of you in the next one."

"How large was the audience?"

"Twelve people, including me and Ted, but I heard that the audience fell off considerably after the reviews appeared."

"It won't happen with the new edition of *The Ladder*." Mrs. Trane nodded with satisfaction.

*   *   *

Lily sat in the cozy living room of Tenisha's apartment. "I throw these revelations from Mrs. Trane into your lap, my practical friend."

"These are matters for a shrink. Purposely slipping on a banana peel is crazy, unless you're a comedian, and she could have imagined the disappearance and reappearance of her bracelet." Tenisha sipped her ginger ale.

"Could have, but I doubt it. Mildred, Suzie Sweet, Roland, they're all expecting too much—money, social position, an ideal wife, an ideal husband. The bracelet incident could be Roland's way of telling his wife that their marriage is over, whether her demands are met or not. He would have access to her jewelry box, and Saks carries his cosmetics line."

"The fact that Roland is financially backing, revising and performing in Mildred's play shows how important the play is to him. Why won't you have some ginger ale?"

"It shows, Ten, that Mildred as a stepping stone is important to him, but it doesn't prove that Mildred as a wife is."

"What did her diary say about the purported push down the stairs?"

"Absolutely nothing."

"That lady has another agenda." Tenisha shook her head and finished her ginger ale.

"She says putting things in writing could be dangerous. Someone could get hold of her diary. What I want to know is whether Mildred Trane is in danger. That's all Bernie wants to know, too. She has at least two male options to replace Roland and says she is willing to consider Row's suggestions, though she's starting with her own. The dinner and play discussion they're hosting at the mansion with

Murdock Pemberton may illuminate the Tranes' personal drama, and I've been invited."

"Well, you're a theater person of sorts. Good luck. I guess you've read about this play of hers. It's in the morning paper." Tenisha thumbed through the newspaper on her coffee table. She pulled out The New York Times theater section, folded it back, smoothed the page flat and plunked it in front of Lily.

MILDRED TRANE TO STAR IN THE LADDER

Lily shook her head sadly. "There are only a handful of people in the audience each night."

"Read on for a critic's thoughts about the play's upcoming debut."

Lily devoured the article quickly. Mildred Trane was going to star in a flop, revised or not. The original backer of the play was allowing would-be playwright, actor and millionaire Roland Trane to revise as well as act in the new production beside his wife.

"Although the principals have kept silent about the changes, spies have revealed that Mr. Trane has made connections with a supernatural twist between the various episodes that chronicle how a man and a woman through various lifetimes, grow or disintegrate, reaping the rewards or punishments due them for their behavior in previous incarnations. The play's revised segments begin in the 1700s and end in current time. Popular fashion designer Bernard Singer will costume the players. *The Ladder*, which is currently available to the audience at no cost, will cost a significant three dollars for the best seats, once beloved theater icon Mildred Trane assumes the major female roles in the play.

"Deemed a disaster at its inception, *The Ladder* has limped along with minimal audiences. Whether deft script revisions, if a new playwright's revisions can possibly be deft, new costumes, and most important, the divine Mildred Trane can resurrect a dead drama and metamorphose it into a resounding success will soon be determined by critics and, of course, fans of Mildred Trane. The play's backer, oil millionaire and philanthropist Edgar B. Davis insists the play's life is worth prolonging. 'This age needs this play,' he says. We shall soon see if 'this age' agrees."

"I don't care how important a client Mildred Trane is, Ten, Bernie is taking a huge risk costuming *The Ladder*. He'll be envied and idolized if the play is a winner, but just because Mildred Trane is in risk mode with Roland doesn't mean Bernie has to jeopardize the reputation of his House this way."

"You are not Bernie's keeper, but he is yours, unless you want to look for another job. Now go home, get dressed and think of the fun we're going to have tonight."

"How can you think of fun at a time like this?"

"Easily."

Chapter Eight

Tenisha threw a light jacket on the sofa in her friend's apartment. "Aren't you ready yet, Lee?"

"I would be, if Bernie hadn't kept me on the phone about delivering a package to Client Number One. It just arrived. We can take care of this en route to Small's Paradise." Lily held up a stunning lavender dress, a Bernard Singer exclusive; it said so on the label. "I told Ted to pick us up at seven o'clock. I'd better hurry. You know how he hates us to be late."

"Hmm. Now time concerns you."

Ted was waiting at the curb with the motor running. "Hi, ladies!" Both he and Donald jumped from the car, Ted to open the door for Lily and Donald to do the same for Tenisha. Lily informed the men of the detour.

"Plenty of time for an eight o'clock reservation," said Ted.

"I'd love to see the inside of the house," said Donald. "I'm taking a course in 19th century English architecture. You can tell a lot about people from their houses. Historically and sociologically, that fascinates me."

"Are you familiar with Willie Simpson? He's one of Mildred Trane's admirers."

"Not personally, Lily, but we're using some of his company's books in the course, one of which he wrote himself, COPYCAT INTERIORS. The Trane mansion was built in 1898, imitating early nineteenth century style."

"We're only stopping by for a few minutes, but maybe the butler will allow a history guru in for a look, Donald."

"Woman's business or not, Lily," countered Donald, "it is a man's house."

"It is," said Lily thoughtfully, "and on loan to wife number three." The look Tenisha gave her silenced her for the rest of the ride. At last Ted pulled into the Trane driveway, and with the early evening moon beaming on all through the Pontiac's windows, he drove onto the gravel parking area thirty feet to the side of the mansion. The butler was not pleased to see four people seeking entrance. He had only been informed of the arrival of one woman, whose destination was madam's boudoir. Lily and Tenisha's familiarity with Mrs. Trane and the magic of the Bernard Singer name persuaded him to let them pass. The men were sternly ordered to follow the butler to the sitting room, Ted in a snit over their treatment and Donald happily ingesting the look of walls, ceilings, art, furniture and carpets. Lily led the front, and Tenisha the train, of Mildred's elegant gown up the circular staircase leading to madam's personal quarters. Lee nodded to the left, and the ladies walked thirty feet with their precious cargo. A faint light shone under the closed bedroom door.

"A welcoming sign," said Lily, as she turned the knob. "Ten!" she screamed, as she hurled the gown to the bed.

Two women were in the room, one being strangled by the other. Lily pinned the attacker's legs together as Tenisha released the assailant's stranglehold on the other woman's neck. The strangler kicked her way free of Lily's grasp and raced through the open door and down the hall. The choking woman emitted a feeble cry, and then, strengthened by horror, sent a powerful shriek resonating through the mansion. Tenisha lowered the woman to the bed, and she and Lily flew down the hall in time to see the assailant careening down the stairs and falling near the bottom. She rose quickly and brushed past three astonished men who attempted to obey Tenisha's call from the top of the stairs: "Hold that woman!" They dashed after her through the front door and into the evening air, but there was no one to be seen or heard, the only sounds being the voices of crickets foreshadowing the night to come. Ted's Pontiac sat alone and silent on the gravel, though a panicked Ted ran to it, suddenly recalling that he had left the key in the ignition. It was still there. Meanwhile, Donald's long legs had mastered the stairs in half a dozen leaps, the elderly butler trailing behind. Tenisha was comforting a sobbing woman.

"What happened? Is she hurt?" asked Donald, but the butler prevented an immediate response as he shouted, "Marie! In Madam's clothes! You have forfeited your position here!"

"Don't be hasty, Roderick," cautioned Tenisha, still holding and consoling the victim. "Madam was meant to be strangled. Marie was the unintended victim. Attacked from the back, the would-be murderer didn't realize it was poor Marie. Mrs. Trane will be grateful. She has been warned."

"Shall I call a doctor?" Roderick asked weakly.

"Please do," said Lily, as Marie, now sitting up on Mrs. Trane's bed, nodded her agreement.

"Such beautiful clothes," the victim gasped between sobs. "I only wanted to try them on."

"You even have your hair in her new bob. Can you act, too? Perhaps this dreadful nightmare will not have been in vain," ventured Lily.

Through her sobs, the young girl gave out with a half laugh. "No, no, but I can dream."

"Yes, of course," Ten replied, "We all can."

Ten and Lee looked at each other. Someone had a dream of a life without Mildred Trane. What woman would that be? Lily bent to the floor to pick something up.

"Good work, Ten. I didn't realize how strong you are."

"In certain neighborhoods of our fair city, self-defense is essential. I didn't always live in a cozy brownstone in a cozy neighborhood with trees painted on the fence." Lily held up strands of brown hair. "No roots," observed Tenisha. "She wore a wig."

Lily nodded. "Or he did. I wonder who else was in the house besides Roderick." The butler in question appeared at that moment announcing that the police were on their way.

"Who else is in the house, Roderick?"

"Why, no one, Miss Chasen."

"And where were you after settling the two gentlemen in the sitting room?"

"Miss!" Roderick was aghast.

"And where will we be when our eight o'clock dinner reservation call goes unanswered?" demanded Ted.

"It's only 7:45," Lily responded innocently.

"Inspector Kirk is on the way," Roderick reiterated. "I can't tell him that I allowed you to leave."

"We can leave without your allowance," said Ted firmly.

"We can chance it," said Lily to Tenisha. "We can deal with the inspector tomorrow."

"What if he shows up?" asked Donald.

"At Teddy's? I doubt it. He hates jazz. The noise, as he calls it, would drive him crazy. He'll wait until tomorrow. The doctor will be here shortly, Marie, so be calm. That's right." Lily patted the girl's hand. "And Roderick, I hope you will not reveal where we are going. Mrs. Trane would not be pleased." Why she wouldn't be pleased, Lily hadn't the slightest idea, but they were off to an evening of dinner, dancing and pleasure—at Small's Paradise!

Chapter Nine

It was midnight, but it could have been mid-day to Lily, so energized was she with the music, the dancing, and, of course, the champagne. She and Tenisha were off work tomorrow; the lateness of the hour would otherwise have verged on the suicidal. She knew it was midnight because she saw several models, Powers girls, making their exit. Their energies and complexions were at stake, and so their departure. The skating waiters for which Small's was famous were nonchalantly delivering appetizers, entrees and desserts. Tenisha poked Lily, who looked toward a corner of the crowded room just as their waiter skated up to the table with coffee and apple pie.

"Joey, do you know the gentleman in that corner with the attractive blonde?" asked Lily.

"Yes, ma'am, I do. He's a regular, Jimmy Carlton. He writes show business reviews and features for *Variety*."

"Do you know who the woman is?"

"No, ma'am. May I get you something else?"

"Yes, Joey, another round of the strongest coffee you've got. We want to stay awake a while longer."

"Amen to that," echoed her tablemates. And Joey skated off.

Lily stared at the couple, Suzie Sweet and Jimmy Carlton, quickly looking away as the pair glanced around the room. "I've read some of Jimmy Carlton's reviews. They're devastating. His nickname is 'Kill Them If You Can Jimmy.' Singers, dancers, actors, he's covered them all with blood. He knows a little about everything and a lot about nothing."

"Why do they keep him on? Oh, I do love Small's apple pie!"

"Because, Ten, he brings in readers. I can't understand why readers enjoy seeing hard-working entertainers destroyed."

"It takes them away from their problems, Lee. 'Misery loves company' has more than a ring of truth to it. I'd wager that he will be *Variety's* reviewer of choice for *The Ladder*."

"For better or worse."

"I'd guess for worse. At least for Roland Trane. A successful Row will make it harder for him to break the link to his wife. Carlton's rare good reviews have almost always been of Mildred Trane performances. I think Suzie Sweet wants to make sure that isn't the case this time."

"But he can still say nice things about her and damn Roland's acting and rewrite, Ten."

"I think Suzie wants her damned as well. If she comes off well, Row may still feel a link to her desirable. He can still be proud to be seen with her, still bask in her glory, very second-hand though it would be."

"Would Carlton do that to a favorite actress, Ten?"

"It's possible. His payoff, they say, is usually the thrill of destruction, and in this case maybe a bit of Suzie Sweet."

As Joey arrived with fresh coffee, Lily pointed to the distant table. "Ever see the young lady with another man?"

"A long time ago."

"Anyone we would know?"

"No one I know. He looked like a businessman to me."

"Roland Trane?" coaxed Tenisha.

"Oh, no, ma'am. I know Mr. Trane. He likes quieter places. He was a regular at my last place. It was too boring for me." And he skated off.

"Husband of Successful Actress Bombs Again in Revised Play," intoned Tenisha. "I can see that, but if Carlton makes them both look bad, sympathy might draw Mildred and Row together. Can't allow that to happen."

"No, Ten. Suzie Sweet has got a problem. Ergo, dinner with Jimmy Carlton to straighten it out. And you're going to have a problem if you finish Donald's apple pie."

Donald looked thoughtfully across the room. "This is social history in the making."

"Another paper you have to write?"

"Why yes, Lily!"

Tenisha was astonished. "Donald, that man could be an accessory in a murder case!"

"Lots of murders in history, too. I might get an interview. Hmm," he pondered. "But I don't want you involved."

"Lots of naive boyfriends in history, too, Donald!"

"I didn't say I'd do anything. I said I might. This would set me apart from other teaching applicants, give me an edge."

"Give you a knife in the back, a plot in a cemetery. Who will your 'edge' impress then?" Tenisha was furious. "What's happened to you, Donald? You used to be so sensible, so conservative!" She pushed the last of Donald's pie away.

Ted cleared his throat. "I think we've all had too much champagne. The coffee should settle our stomachs and our minds. Drink up, and let's go home."

Ted and Donald split the bill, and the two couples made their way slowly past the closely packed tables to the door. Looking ahead to the entrance, Lily saw a girl not more than nineteen and a distinguished-looking gentleman waiting to be seated. Lily stopped short, causing someone behind her to slam into her back.

"I must sit for a moment; there's a tear in my stocking."

"But we're going home," said Ted.

"What can we do about it here?" said Donald.

Tenisha's eyes followed Lily's. The couple at the entrance was on the move now. They were about to be seated. What to do! The man was Roland Trane.

"Only a minute, darling," said Ted.

"Guaranteed," added Donald, as the men headed towards the cloakroom to get their wraps. Lily glanced at the cloakroom line. Ted and Donald would be at least another three or four minutes. A bluff was in order. She approached the maitre d'.

"Excuse me, I'd love to know how Mr. Trane could call so late and still get a reservation for tonight."

The maitre d' squared his shoulders. "We don't play favorites here. The reservation was made a week ago."

"Ah, but a lot can happen in a week."

"The lady reconfirmed last evening. Excuse me." And he huffed off in the grand manner suitable to the ruler of a popular domain. Ted and Donald returned and helped the ladies on with their coats. Lily and Tenisha moved to the right of a line of people waiting to be seated.

"What are you doing?" Ted and Donald asked in unison.

"A play is about to begin," said Lily.

"And it's not one we want to miss," added Tenisha.

"I have to be at work early tomorrow," said Ted.

"I have to go to school," said Donald.

"We have to stay," chorused Lily and Tenisha.

The men scrunched their faces, folded their arms and glared at their women.

In the corner, Suzie Sweet, now aware of the dreaded entrance, pulled back from Jimmy Carlton. She offered her hand and a few words. He departed quickly. Suzie Sweet rose, and using her arms to ward off dancing and entering patrons, headed straight toward Roland Trane. Her words could not be heard above the din of voices and music, but her gestures were unmistakable.

The bouncer was hailed by the alert maitre d'.

"Great movie material," said Tenisha. "She'd better get in before the talkies take control."

Roland had stood up. His frightened date had not. He was trying to reason with Miss Sweet. Seeing the futility of this, he took the elbow of the seated lady, got her up and headed toward the exit, with Sweet shouting and flailing her arms right behind them. The maitre d' had their coats at the ready, and they took them and hurried away, the broad-chested bouncer blocking Suzie's exit until, at a sign from his boss, he stepped aside to a barrage of invective, as an outraged Sweet stormed out.

"See? We were only delayed ten minutes," said Tenisha to their stunned escorts.

Chapter Ten

"Has no one ever told you, Miss Chasen, that you don't leave the scene of a crime?"

"If you're the criminal, you do, Inspector Kirk."

"Miss Chasen!"

"I didn't think you'd need me until morning, at least."

"I decide whether I need to talk to someone about an attempted murder, and I decide when. I notice you didn't rush to see me this morning with your side of the story."

"I have a job, Inspector, and how many sides of the story are there?"

"I'll know after I've questioned everyone. Now, tell me in your own words what happened."

Lily wasn't sure whose words he thought she might use, but she didn't comment on it. She described their arrival, the stranglehold, the scream, the kick and the escape. The inspector seemed disappointed.

"Same story as the others?" she asked.

"You're a model. You're supposed to be aware of details."

Lily promptly described the style and pattern of the dress the maid had borrowed from Mildred Trane's closet.

"Thank you," said the inspector, slamming his dime store pen so hard into his writing pad that it split in half, spewing ink in several directions, including his own. Lily grabbed some tissues to assist in cleaning his person. "Stop that! And where did you go after the crime? And don't tell me Teddy's."

"Of course not, Inspector. I told Roderick not to tell you that. Young women are entitled to some privacy of an evening. Was the poor victim able to tell you anything?"

"You know she couldn't, or she would have told you. I have no doubt that you asked. I suggest you mind your own business and allow professionals to do their work without interference."

Lily looked thoughtful. Was the would-be murderer a hired professional or a desperate amateur?

"Have you remembered something, Miss Chasen?"

"No, I was just thinking."

"Well stop thinking of anything but fashion! Good day!"

Tenisha entered the salon. "You didn't tell him we're investigating per Bernie's instructions, per Mildred's instructions?"

"He didn't ask, so I didn't have to lie. It's a good thing we came to work this morning, or he would have asked what our time-out was for."

"What did he ask you, Ten?"

"What happened and why we were there. He said he had asked Roderick where the Tranes were, and that loyal Rock of Gibralter said he didn't know. The inspector used the mansion telephone to call their places of work. No one responded at Trane & Co. At the theater, the night watchman said the theater was closed, whereabouts of party unknown. He then telephoned every nightclub in the city, but neither Trane could be located."

"They wouldn't use their own names. Even Joey didn't know that Roland Trane would be at Small's Paradise last night."

"That young lady Roland Trane was with certainly looked frightened when the big, bad 'Sweet' wolf slammed Roland at the table."

"If he had known what she was concocting with Jimmy Carlton, he could have slammed right back. Roland has a history of dating theater women, not innocents. That young lady may not have been a date at all, not in the usual sense of the term. If we're going to wrap up this Trane business quickly, as Bernie and the star expect, we ought to discover who the girl is."

"The club won't tell you, Lee."

"No, but Joey might. Sweet kid, and I've got front and center tickets for Thursday's big basketball game. Remember, the maitre d' said the girl confirmed the day before. The reservation must have been in her name. The club won't tell the police. They'll protect a patron's privacy, especially when she's accompanied by a high-profile person like Roland Trane, and they won't have to lie, either. The police will never think to ask who made the reservation. They'll assume it was Roland. I hear rehearsals run late, but the police will be able to question Mildred Trane tonight. She's got a costume fitting here tomorrow. I'll call Uncle Harry when I get home. I'm sure Inspector Kirk isn't bugging his telephone line. I wouldn't want him to think Harry Chasen is helping us, as he did last year in the Lizette Frere case. Uncle Harry has five more years on the police force before retirement. Since Kirk has already spoken to Ted and Donald, we have some breathing space. The inspector should not be bothering us for at least twenty-four hours."

"Donald really shocked me last night, Lee."

"He was protective of you, Ten. No shock in that. As for being intrigued by attempted murder, well, murder is heady stuff. He'll get over it. There are safer ways to show he'd make an excellent teacher. You know what he's really like. Oh yes, you do!"

Chapter Eleven

"I thought your parents were dead."

"Well, they're not. At least, Mother isn't. Thank you for agreeing to see me, and on such short notice." Roland Trane sat awkwardly on the showroom sofa, framed in afternoon sunlight.

"It was very brave of you to ask me," said Lily. "If your wife or Miss Sweet find out about this meeting, your explanations to both will have to be inspired."

"You and your date saw me at Small's last night, and I know that you're Mildred's favorite model, and that she has trusted you with more than clothes. I wanted to set your mind, and by extension hers, at ease about that event."

"What makes you think our relationship goes deeper than clothes?"

"I'm not a total idiot, partial perhaps, but not total. I know she comes here when she has no fittings, viewings or other fashion business to conduct. I'm reasonably good at simple arithmetic."

"Set my mind at ease, then." Lily leaned back in her chair.

"My mother visits me annually. She lives quietly near Cannes in a country cottage with my sister. When she and Father divorced twenty years ago, Father took charge of me, and she took Vivian, who was only one at the time, to France. They settled where they now live, a stone's throw from a convent which offers early childhood training and a middle school. A private all-girls college is an hour away, and Vivian completed her studies there. Mother felt that I was beyond redemption. I was too much like Father, but she believed that the surprise birth of her second child when she was forty-six

43

gave her a second chance to 'get it right,' as she put it, and rear a child who would make her proud. But she has not abandoned me. Every year she comes to check out me and my lifestyle. During the year, she is not to be contacted, except for emergencies. Vivian and I have exchanged birthday cards, but otherwise, there has been no contact between us. Mother has not wanted me to affect her in any way. Since I married Mother's favorite actress and stayed married to her for ten years, she was beginning to change her mind. Vivian has read heaps about Mildred, and Mother would like them to meet, but with Mildred about to exit my life, apart from the play, of course, I'm not sure it's a good idea. I took my sister to Small's because I thought she'd enjoy it, and because I wanted her to understand what I'm doing."

"And what do you want of me?"

"I want you to understand what I'm not doing and relay it to Mildred. When I try, my blood pressure soars. Specifically, I want you to tell her to stop implying that I'm out to kill her, and that I've had affairs with several women over the course of our marriage. Her allegations have no legal standing but may be harmful to me in a circumstantial way, in the situation of our housemaid, for example."

"Are you saying, then, that you have not tried to have her killed and have not had affairs during the course of your marriage?"

"No, I'm not saying that. I'm saying that such unprovable allegations can be damaging to my reputation and career."

"And your wife's divorce settlement."

"To put it bluntly, yes."

"You would, of course, retain your family attorney, and your wife would have to find an attorney for herself."

Roland Trane hesitated. "Our attorney hasn't decided which party he will represent."

"But he's willing to represent one of you."

"Yes."

"I'll tell your wife what you've said. I can offer no opinion of my own. But you should be telling her this yourself."

"We're not presently on speaking terms. At dinner tomorrow night, we will be speaking on business matters. That's different."

Is it? wondered Lily, as she rose to answer a call to model in one of Bernie's private showings.

* * *

Donald flexed his shoulders, gripped the bowling ball, pulled it back slowly, and let fly with a shot that sent it down the alley for a strike.

"Meticulous and accurate," said Tenisha proudly, as Ted approached the lane.

"Marital relations can really be a puzzle," said Lily to Tenisha. "Once upon a time, Roland loved Mildred, and got enough out of their marriage to stick with it for ten years, and now he thinks her mercenary and vindictive. She loved him enough to marry him, says she wants another like him, except in the matter of skirt-chasing, but is afraid he wants to kill her. Can husbands and wives fake a good relationship for ten years and then discover that they didn't truly understand the other party?"

"People get older, Lee. Their perspectives change, and their fears, too." She hugged Donald as he returned from his successful play, watching as he riveted his attention on Ted, who threw a spare. Donald breathed a sigh of relief.

"Being old, alone and poor isn't something uplifting to contemplate, but Mildred Trane is decades away from that possible ending to her story."

"Some stories end sooner than others, Lee, and actresses like to know the end of the play. Naturally, men are forever desirable, especially when their bank accounts are full."

Lily laughed, as she rose, picked up a bowling ball and headed to the lane.

Chapter Twelve

"**D**on't you think murder a rather severe punishment for infidelity?" Director Murdock Pemberton looked at the snail on his fork, and then at Roland Trane, sitting across from him in the dining room of the Trane mansion.

"I think that man's behavior through the centuries has been building towards his exit in a dramatic manner." Mrs. Trane concentrated on buttering her roll. "Jim Davis's original script and all your subsequent versions have insisted that virtue be rewarded and immorality punished. Edgar Davis has spent a fortune keeping the play alive because he sees it as a moral lesson and a warning. A confrontation with death gives one pause, encourages one to reflect on the relationship between fiction and fact, between the drama on stage and the drama in one's life."

"An accident, Roland, a prophetic accident, would send the same message in a more discreet, yet obvious way, a more drama-worthy way, don't you think?"

"You think too well of theatergoers today, Murdock. Subtlety often eludes the debauched, the worldly-minded, as witness the response of critics as well as your audience numbers for the past two years."

A faint flush appeared on the director's cheeks. "The right audience, the educated, alert audience that Mildred will attract will understand and appreciate the subtleties, and go forth to spread the word, to form, as it were, an informal social revolution, to redeem those lost to the iniquities of this modern age. This is a drama that can affect society, change individual lives. It's so important, such a vital social service that I've agreed to direct another man's script of a play I spent so much time writing and rewriting myself. I'm thrilled with the supernatural element with which you've infused the drama. The message is not merely a worldly corrective, it is a spiritual corrective, and you've zeroed in on that superbly and given the play the vital dimension it lacked. But I hesitate at the murder."

"Would that everyone would hesitate at murder," murmured Mildred Trane.

"Is there not, perhaps, another way to dispatch the character? Why endanger the future of a decent human being meting out illegal, though deserved, justice?" Pemberton's eyes boring into Roland Trane's indicated that this was a dare.

For a moment there was silence, as all looked into outer space, or rather the space beyond the table where the maid had begun setting the dessert plates at each diner's elbow. Mildre Trane was the first to speak.

"Suicide, perhaps," she said. "Self-inflicted punishment by a man who at last recognized his misspent centuries and was ready to atone by preventing the reoccurrence in future centuries and putting a satisfying moral conclusion to his behavior."

"'Bravo, Mildred, or should I say, 'Brava.'" Murdock Pemberton nodded in Lily's direction.

"What do you say, Roland?"

Roland Trane narrowed his eyes as he looked at his wife. "Do you think our man capable of suicide?"

"Oh, yes, most definitely yes," she replied.

Roland Trane was silent for a very long time. "It shall be done. It's rather early in the play, but it shall be done. This requires no changes in your lines, Mildred, only in mine."

"No change at all," she affirmed.

The director clapped his hands in delight and, as if it were a signal, coffee was served.

*   *   *

"I know the revised *Ladder* has had plenty of attic rehearsal time, but I hope the brief rehearsal time at the theater was enough. The play re-opens in three days. How are we progressing, ladies?" asked Bernard Singer.

Be optimistic, Bernie had said, be optimistic. Failing that, Lily turned to Mildred Trane, sitting legs crossed on the sofa in Singer's office. "What have the police said?"

"They're stuck in 'Row' mode. They said only a man could have so strong a grip, and only Roland would know his way so well around the house to conveniently get lost in it. But we can't have any of that."

Bernard Singer vigorously shook his head in agreement.

No, thought Lily. We insist on an outcome that does not implicate the husband of Favored Client Number One. Assuming he was hidden somewhere on the premises at the time, the only man in the house, besides the butler, would have been Roland. Roderick didn't have the strength to strangle anyone or the fleetness of foot to escape so quickly. A woman could have donned a wig, so the cook and housemaids could have been under suspicion, but they weren't, probably because they had no motives. A cash payment could have been a motive, but after ten years of loyal service, Inspector Kirk apparently didn't think it likely, and neither did Lily.

"The inspector is questioning others, but not with much fervor, Lily."

"Others, Mrs. Trane? Such as?"

"Publisher Willie Simpson and construction engineer Robert Blair."

"They're on your spousal trial list. What about the men on Roland's spousal list?"

"Roland's list is a work in progress, with no progress to date. That is another reason the inspector is suspicious of my darling. If I no longer existed, says the good inspector, then the agony of Roland's mate selection and certain rejection by me could be avoided. How dare he impugn my motives! I said I would consider Roland's prospective husbands, and I would!

"The jaundiced inspector also says that my demise would eliminate a hefty divorce settlement, probably for life, if my attorney has his way. He believes that William Branten is already looking for loopholes to enlarge the prenuptial agreement. Is there a bitterness requirement to attain the rank of inspector? Perhaps we should write the inspector into *The Ladder* and eliminate him!

"He says that Roland believes I have no intention of agreeing to a divorce. Roland has not told me that. He's treating my request with respect."

"As he should!" interjected Singer.

It's more of a demand, thought Lily. "But the two of you are not speaking, apart from *Ladder* business."

"That's because the inspector is feeding Roland innuendos, personal feelings and downright lies and, temporarily at least, Row seems to be believing them."

"You have your husband committing suicide in the play."

"It's only in the play. A play is a play. Its purpose is to divert your attention from reality. Roland is quite fit and can look forward to a long life."

"Your director equates *The Ladder* with real life, and you said that the theme of the play was what appealed to you: final justice for deeds done in various incarnations."

"One mustn't take fiction too literally." Mildred Trane crossed her legs away from Lily. "What have you discovered since our dinner?"

"Yes, Lee," said Singer eagerly. "We need information that will end our anguish quickly."

"That Suzie Sweet has jeopardized her standing with Roland and that his mother is determined to continue as your mother-in-law. His sister, who has been advised for twenty-one years by her mother and the nuns, has undoubtedly given him saintly, cautionary advice that should reinforce the status quo."

"His sister, here? And Mother Trane has already arrived?"

"Yes, indeed. Your husband undoubtedly wanted to talk to them before you did."

"Set the stage, you mean, for his point of view." Mildred Trane stood and started pacing the room. "But if Miss Sweet has behaved badly, would that be necessary?"

"Miss Sweet behaved badly because she misjudged Vivian when she saw her with her brother at Small's Paradise last night. Tenisha and I were there and witnessed her display of temper. Your sister-in-law was badly frightened by Miss Sweet."

"Stupid woman!"

"Your husband came to Singer Couture yesterday to ask me to relay a message to you, since you're not conversing. He believes you're trying to get him accused of attempted murder, and he wants you to stop."

"That's crazy! I want to stay married to him!"

"I suggest you try convincing him of that."

"Do you believe it?"

"I have no beliefs in the matter. My sole interest is in facts. You're holding your patronage at Singer Couture over our heads to get your way in your personal interests. Tenisha Jones and I are either investigating a murder plot or a mirage. We haven't determined which."

Bernard Singer jumped up, horrified. "Lee, how dare you speak that way to Mrs. Trane!"

Mildred Trane ignored the couturier. "I say it's a murder plot! I do not perform in fairy tales!"

"Perform?

"Play-act. I will continue to purchase from Bernie whether you help me or not, unless I'm not alive, and therefore not in a position to do so."

"I apologize, Mrs. Trane. I had to hear you respond emotionally, not mentally."

"Apology accepted. I trust you. I don't know why, but there's something about you that encourages trust, whether in the end you can help me or not."

Bernard Singer mopped his sweating brow.

"Thank you, Mrs. Trane. It's probably because I sing."

Chapter Thirteen

"Lunch with my favorite uncle? Of course, darling. Well, you'd be my favorite even if the others did live in New York City. Oh, I love the Roosevelt Grill! Why will you be in a sports jacket? Oh, you're on a case. Somebody who would be suspicious at the Grill? No? Well, that's good. And you needn't worry. I won't be grilling you for information about the inspector's suspicions or findings in the Trane case. It's not much of a case anyway—suspicions of a thwarted wife, strayings of a devoted husband. We won't talk about it. Oh, we will talk about it." Lily put the telephone receiver to the other ear. "But I thought you weren't allowed to give me information. What do you mean you want me to give you information? Well, how nice that the inspector is willing to allow it! I'm sure he knows as much about her as I do, probably much more. Hasn't he questioned her? Well, it's not too late. Oh, it is too late." Lily was silent as she listened to Uncle Harry. She nodded at the telephone. "Lunch at noon." Lily looked up at Tenisha as she replaced the receiver. "Suzie Sweet has been murdered."

Harry Chasen was already seated at a corner table when Lily and Tenisha entered the restaurant, which Lee found as comfortable as an old glove, but eminently more stylish.

"Two pairs of eyes and ears are better than one, Uncle Harry, so I asked Tenisha to join us, since she was at Small's when Miss Sweet was there." Lily kissed her uncle on the cheek, and Tenisha shook his hand. "Surely you've checked Miss Sweet's background."

"Of course, dear. No old boyfriends who would avenge her loss to Roland. She's been seeing Roland Trane for two years, mostly secretly, but she bragged; all the dancers knew. None of them in the same professional league as Mildred Trane's colleagues. We checked with them. They weren't aware of the affair until recently."

"Not too likely, then, that they would have waited until now to dispatch her out of loyalty to Mrs. Trane, and not too likely that Sweet's friends, male especially, would have waited this long to avenge losing her to Big Money," said Tenisha.

"The inspector's thinking exactly," said Uncle Harry.

Tenisha looked deflated. It was well-meant, but hardly a compliment. Harry Chasen looked at the drink list, lingering on the beer column. He sighed. Not while he was on duty. "Lily, Tenisha, what we want to know is—who was Miss Sweet with? Have you any idea what they were talking about, and did you recognize anyone else at Small's who would know her or the party she was with?"

"She was with Jimmy Carlton, Uncle Harry, and we have no idea of what they were talking about, except the obvious, something for *Variety*. Her career? Not too likely, unless he's doing a column on anonymous chorus line dancers. More likely it's about her boyfriend's new project, career, or whatever, in some way a link to Carlton's favorite actress, Mildred Trane."

"That's more likely, Lily. We'll have to talk to him. Hope he'll be honest. You never know with fans of one part of a triangle." Chasen looked at his watch. "Sorry, ladies, I have to go." He motioned to the waiter and paid the check. "Finish your lunch. I'll drop by tonight, Lily."

"Mildred Trane must have been shocked to learn that Roland's deception was long-term."

"Maybe not, Ten. Disappointed, I'm sure, but if rumor is correct, he's had flings before. But after ten years, would the latest in an ongoing series push her to murder? I don't think so. She'd need a stronger, more immediate reason."

"What about Mildred Trane hopefuls?"

"What do you mean, Ten?"

"What if the death of Suzie Sweet brings Mildred Trane to her senses, to the realization that it's merely one more down and who knows how many more to go, that it's time for her to leave, while comparative youth is on her side, rather than delay and get tossed. Notice, she didn't wait for him to compile a list of eligibles. She started exploring on her own."

"With very unlikely prospects, Ten."

"Are they? An amusing, witty publisher with classic homes expertise, and a boring construction engineer, hardly like Roland, but if a woman is willing to settle for a permanent arrangement in which she is amused without being threatened or bored by someone who will not stray, she might feel free to seek emotional satisfaction elsewhere."

"You mean, Ten, to feel free to do as she likes, to sample admirers without fear of commitment, the marriage commitment acting as her defense. I wonder if this is what Roland has done for a chunk of their marriage! Was he ever in love with Mildred, or with a star and her aura? But would a conservative, proper Mildred Trane do such a thing?"

"Dear Lee, we've seen a prize client use that position to bend Bernie to her will and get us involved to protect her, or is it to bolster an alibi should a Roland Trane amoureux suddenly die? We've seen an actress use power and at least one lie—remember that banana peel—to get her way. Human relations are meat and potatoes to an actress known and admired for her convincing, serious roles. Convincing and serious, Lee."

"And she's the great favorite of Jimmy Carlton. Could he be bent to her will? I'd wager that her chance of success in doing that would be greater than Suzie Sweet's, if Carlton thought Sweet's proposal would harm Mildred in any way, and as Mildred's adversary for Roland's affections, it very well might. Carlton has interviewed Mildred during the run of all her plays, and beyond. He knows her better than Suzie did. Maybe even more than that. He's married with children, but when has that ever stopped a man—we have to talk to him."

"Inspector Kirk will be doing that."

"And I'll find out tonight from Uncle Harry what the police know. The inspector is a man of science, not of the arts. His interest in theater is nil, but the theater is a reflection of life, of people, of the human heart."

"Mildred is the obvious suspect for the murder of Suzie Sweet."

"And the attempt on her life via her maid?"

"A ruse, they'll say. She's strong, works out daily at the gym, can disappear as no one else can from her premises."

"So, Ten, Roland would be free to find another Suzie Sweet, or a plethora of them. But who could prop up his self-esteem as reliably as Mildred has for ten years? Of course, if his part in *The Ladder* or his rewrite of the play, or both, are successful, he may feel he'll be fine on his own. The demise of Suzie Sweet spares him the angst of another failed relationship. He would be free of both women, and his wealth would be intact. Mildred would get a fortune in a divorce."

"So, either one of them would find a long-term benefit in disposing of the other. Buzz me when Uncle Harry leaves, but not after eight. Dinner with Donald." Tenisha took a final bite of the mousse, eyed the slice Lily had left and cleaned the plate, accompanied by her friend's musical laughter.

*　*　*

Uncle Harry patted the cushion on the sofa, and his niece joined him.

"Well, favorite uncle, what was Jimmy Carlton's story?"

"You know, dear, that as a Mildred Trane fan he would be interested in anything to do with her, so Suzie Sweet tried to persuade him to write derogatory comments about Roland's contributions to the revised *Ladder*. She said he would be doing Mildred Trane a favor because she deserves better than a wandering husband, and, if free, she would find someone worthy of her stature and character. Of course, she noted, she, Suzie, would also benefit, acquiring a wealthy husband, if only temporarily, but she was used to being bought and tossed, while Mrs. Trane was not. She respected the actress and wished her well. Mr. Carlton need only consider the benefit to Mildred Trane. Since Roland Trane's imminent divorce of his wife has not been made public yet, Carlton was shocked to hear of it. He doubted the veracity of this report, but Miss Sweet assured him that she and Mr. Trane were to be married. She mentioned that Roland is compiling a list of potential suitors for his wife, but that

Mrs. Trane is also exploring potential mates on her own. He said it took him some minutes to absorb this information, which was so detailed he thought there might be some truth to it. He said that Roland's behavior deserved to be slammed, but that any derogatory elements in his review of *The Ladder* would be only of work onstage, including Mildred's. He regretted that his reputation as a mean-spirited reviewer is so widespread. He feels it is unjust. Quality plays and performances are too rare these days. He insists he will be fair regardless of what others think. He admitted, though, that when Roland entered Smalls with an unfamiliar young lady, he shuddered and said, 'What a horrible man.'"

"Uncle Harry, you would have made a great lawyer. Your stories are always so detailed."

"You should hear the one about the matron who had her eye on me, both eyes unfortunately, and fell into the arms of the prisoner she was escorting to the dock. But that's for another time. You know, baby, one lawyer in the family is enough. I love your dad, but his work is all cerebral. Mine is interlaced with action. I can move around, and I don't have to knock off twenty pounds."

"Mom says Dad's sticking to his diet."

"That's good. Walt's a great guy. I'm glad he's enjoying his life with your fabulous mom up in Rochester, where he's out of my hair."

"Uncle Harry!"

"Advice, advice, advice! I can bear it on the telephone. So, is there anything more you can tell me about Suzie Sweet?"

"No, darling, that was the first time I saw her. She was needlessly furious with Roland."

"We had to interview Roland's sister. He was upset, but he understood. We also spoke to their mother. An annual trek to New York doesn't qualify them as murder suspects. They've barely had time to get their bearings. A luggage mix-up. The airline just delivered their luggage this morning. And now this." His outstretched hands encompassed the murder and everything radiating from it.

"Thanks, Uncle Harry. You know, you'd make some lucky woman luckier. You've been alone too long."

"Single, unattached, but not alone. But those are stories for another time."

"Funny how 'another time' never comes."

Harry Chasen laughed heartily. "Give Tenisha my love, and tell her not to be too upset with me. I'll be talking to Donald to see the Small's episode through his eyes. I guess Ted told you I spoke to him this morning."

"Yes. Sorry he couldn't add anything to what Tenisha and I told you."

"That's all right. Little bits and pieces added to other information can open new avenues for investigation. You never know."

"All right, darling. It's almost eight o'clock, and you've only had orange juice, so I deduce you've got a personal 'story' waiting for your arrival, for dinner and dancing, perhaps?"

Harry Chasen pinched his niece's cheek. "You should have been a detective. Oh, excuse me, you are!" He hugged Lily and left.

Bits and pieces, thought Lily. You never know where they can lead. She went to the telephone and dialed Tenisha's number. "Tonight? Well, bring him over too. I need four brilliant heads working on a puzzle. Just for an hour. You can continue your date wherever you like after."

For the next twenty minutes, Lily Chasen was on the telephone. She never thought she would get so much use out of this instrument she had been so loath to buy, and which her parents, fearful for her safety in the city, had sent her as a gift. When Tenisha and Donald arrived, Ted was already present, and lemon merengue pie, not usual fare for a model, was on the table, with a pot of coffee and a pot of tea on either side of it.

Bolstered by the pie, Lily felt it safe to begin. "What did you think of Jimmy Carlton's behavior at Small's?"

"He was leaning back in his chair," said Tenisha, "not forward into the speaker, as someone would who was getting confidential information. Could also have been a sign of distrust of Suzie Sweet."

"He didn't seem emotionally involved," said Donald. "He looked relaxed."

"He left in a hurry," added Ted. "It looked like he alerted Suzie Sweet that Roland had entered. He was facing the entry. She was not. Roland would certainly recognize her, but would he recognize Carlton?"

"Even if he didn't yet, he would after Carlton's review of the play was published."

"No, Donald. Carlton's picture does not accompany his column. He might be a dead or mangled Jimmy Carlton by now, if all the theater folk whose lives he's damaged knew what he looked like. His official photograph has him sporting a mustache. If Suzie had to explain that her date was a reporter, she'd have to explain more than she would like. Carlton wouldn't be in trouble with Roland, but Suzie would be. Carlton's interviewed Mildred Trane each time she's been in a play, always in a public place."

"A wise precaution, Lee, if the man's married with children."

"It would certainly look safe, Ten, but remember what you said about Suzie Sweet's possible deal with Carlton? That he might get a bit of Miss Sweet too?"

"You're implying something foreign to Mildred Trane."

"Maybe I am, Ten, but it's something we should look into. Not everything about Mildred Trane is in the open. Certainly her looming divorce —"

"You mean Roland's divorce of her."

"Yes, certainly, that's not known yet. It's time to explore the Carlton-Trane relationship. It might be quite professional and innocent. If so, we might still stumble upon a 'bit' or 'piece' that will move our investigation along."

"Investigation! Serious stuff! Well, whatever you call it, Lee, we've got Bernie's deadline, which is actually Mildred Trane's deadline, before the on-stage drama begins."

"If you don't meet the deadline, the world won't end," offered Donald.

"No," said Lily, "but somebody's life might. There's a lot of money riding on our off-stage drama."

Chapter Fourteen

"Bernie will have a fit, Lee," warned Tenisha.

"Maybe so, but we've got to speak to Jimmy Carlton ourselves, and this is the best excuse I could think of." Lily lifted the portfolio out of Ted's Pontiac. "Pick us up in an hour and a half, Ted. That should give us plenty of time."

"Okay, honey, but be careful."

"We're' safe, Ted, don't worry. It's broad daylight, and we're at the offices of a well-known publication."

"I'm more concerned about what you'll say. Words have power. Be careful what you say and how you say it."

Lily blew Ted a kiss, Tenisha waved, and they entered the precincts of *Variety*.

"Mr. Carlton. We have a two o'clock appointment. Lily Chasen and Tenisha Jones."

"Just a moment, please." The receptionist checked her book and announced their arrival. "You may go in. First door on your right."

Jimmy Carlton came out from behind his desk to shake their hands. "You asked for a clarification meeting. Well, by all means, clear away."

"Mr. Singer thought it important for you to understand why he chose the fabrics he did for *The Ladder*, their significance in the plot and their suitability for the various actors. We'll arrange them in chronological order in the play." Lily began her explanation, while Tenisha pulled out succeeding fabrics, remarking on the styles of the various eras, and how her boss had adapted the fabrics to them in his creations.

"Washable, you say. No need for the cleaners. Yes, of course. Worn daily for months, perhaps longer, they would have to survive in reasonable shape for as low a cost as possible. So, Mr. Davis is expecting a long run, I take it, one he won't have to continue to subsidize."

"That's the idea, Mr. Carlton."

"And a good one. But is the revised play a good one? That we shall soon determine."

"You'll come with an open mind, I'm sure. Mrs. Trane is not in the habit of performing in unworthy plays," said Lily.

"True, Miss Chasen, but when one's husband is involved in a production, the wife may turn a blind eye to its defects."

"Since the marriage is nearing its end, Mrs. Trane can be objective about the revised play's quality."

"You know about that? I thought that information was not to be revealed until well into the presumed success of the play."

"Mrs. Trane told me that she told Inspector Kirk, who told you, so it's not a secret to those of us in this room, Mr. Carlton."

"Mildred is taking a big chance if she thinks a successful *Ladder* will allow her to keep Roland, but she took a big chance marrying him ten years ago. I can't think of another established actress who would change her name to her husband's. But she got away with it. Her marriage lasted, and her fame continued under the Trane logo, increased even, with men and women alike. Very conservative, her audiences. She was respected for becoming 'the little woman' to the big man, when actually the saying should have been reversed. She thought the name change would add permanency to their marriage, and it did add ten years, but hardly 'till death do us part.' Maybe she thinks *The Ladder* will add another ten years. Maybe as Roland gets older and his desserts get younger, his doctor will tell him enough, although a fatal heart attack would give their marriage permanency and a respectable ending."

"You seem to know a lot about how Mrs. Trane thinks."

Jimmy Carlton sighed. "I've interviewed her at least a dozen times, Miss Jones. You get to know someone, to like someone that way. She's been honest with me, and I've kept her thoughts private."

"Until now."

"She's confided in you, Miss Chasen, or I wouldn't have. Her life is about to blow up anyway. Truth tends to do that eventually. And if it doesn't just yet, I'm sure you ladies will preserve her privacy, as well as her patronage at Singer Couture."

"Have you spoken to Mrs. Trane about *The Ladder*?" asked Lily. Carlton sat erect and answered quickly. "If you check my backlog of interviews with her, you'll see that the last one was two years ago."

"I didn't mean a published interview, Mr. Carlton. Despite being an objective reviewer, you are a long-time friend of Mrs. Trane. Surely, you've spoken between plays. Did you, perhaps, advise her to do the six-month run in London's West End two years ago?"

Jimmy Carlton looked down at his desk. "She didn't ask me," he said softly.

"As a friend, did you make a suggestion anyway?"

Carlton's eyes probed Lily's for a moment. "It was a good play, but I didn't think it wise to leave America at that time."

"Do you mean to leave Roland?"

"Playwrights and producers were practically breaking down her door with interesting opportunities, but—yes, Roland, too."

"Mrs. Trane is an extremely astute and alert lady," said Tenisha. "How could you know more about her life than she?"

Jimmy Carlton shrugged. "I just did."

"And she didn't want to believe you?"

"Mildred Trane believes me. I've never lied to her, and she knows it."

"Then London's West End was a test?"

Carlton smiled. "A test, Miss Jones." He thumbed through *The Ladder*'s fabrics. "And now she's stuck with the results."

"You understand relationships; you understand marriage. Your wife is a lucky woman."

"Thank you, Miss Chasen, but understanding isn't enough. Acting on that understanding is equally important. My wife is lucky, indeed."

"A teeny bit boastful, are we?" teased Lily.

"No, Miss Chasen, not boastful at all. Now, I will certainly keep Mr. Singer's role in *The Ladder* in mind, and my kudos will be in print, should kudos be warranted. Is there anything else you feel I should know before trumpets sound and the new *Ladder* takes its place in history?"

"No. We thank you, and Mr. Singer thanks you." Lily glanced at her watch. "Right on time. My boyfriend is picking us up in three minutes. His father's firm, Walter Martin Fabrics, supplied the material for the costumes."

"Oh, then I must mention him too," said Jimmy Carlton.

Ted's car was at the curb as the women exited *Variety*. "Praise all around," said Tenisha, leaning back in the Pontiac, "for fabric and costume designer alike, for them at least, even if *The Ladder* number two is a flop."

"A successful visit, then, ladies?"

"Informative," said Lily, "and information can lead to…"

"The grocery, Lee. You're short of milk, remember?"

"Thanks, Ten. I'll just—my purse! Oh dear, I left my purse on Carlton's desk. Ted—"

"I'll drive you back tomorrow before you go to work. Call Carlton when you get home. We're almost there. How much money do you need?"

"No, Ted. Now, please. I need my keys."

"Doesn't that sweet, old man downstairs hold your spare key?"

"Yes, but he doesn't hold my address book."

Ted looked puzzled, but Tenisha said, "Ah!" If Carlton looked at it to get her number listed on the front, he might also see telephone numbers she should not have if her business were only fashion-related, like Uncle Harry's and Inspector Kirk's. It was the end of a working day for most, and the streets were filling with automobiles, and the sidewalks were getting crowded.

"I hope he hasn't left yet," said Lily, scrambling out of the vehicle without waiting for Ted to open her door, leaving him standing on the street looking foolish.

Lily shouted, "Mr. Carlton!" as the writer walked behind Ted's Pontiac, intent on crossing the street. Suddenly her eyes widened, and she screamed, "Look out!" to an unheeding Carlton.

In a flash, Ted was at the rear of his car. He pushed Carlton toward the sidewalk, out of the path of an onrushing vehicle, and fell on top of him. Lily rushed to both men as Ted stood upright.

"Carlton's hurt!" she shouted. "Get an ambulance!"

Tenisha had already entered *Variety* to do just that.

"Are you all right, Ted?"

"Yes, cushioned by Carlton. There was nothing else I could do."

"Mr. Carlton, Mr. Carlton, can you hear me?" cried Lily to the unconscious man, as Ted parted the writer's hair to reveal a swelling.

"He hit his head. Fortunately, it didn't strike the concrete," said Ted. He looked at the square plot of soil beneath the silent man, and then up at what was rooted in it. "The tree of life," he said. "It sure saved his."

Tenisha was now at their side, and an ambulance could be heard in the distance. As it pulled parallel to Ted's car, the trio moved out of the way. The EMS technicians laid the stretcher on the ground. Several *Variety* employees were on the sidewalk now, and a police car pulled up behind the ambulance.

"We're going with him," chorused Lily and Tenisha, as Inspector Kirk slammed his car door and approached them.

"Oh no, you're not."

"We know him. We just spent an hour and a half talking to him."

"He's unconscious. He can't say anything to you busybodies. You'll come with me in the police car. You too, Mr. Martin."

"I'm not leaving my car! I dropped the ladies off and just came back to pick them up. When I saw a vehicle rushing toward Mr. Carlton, I pushed him out of the way."

"All right, I'll call you tonight."

"Yes, sir. Lily, I'll get the milk and leave it with Mr. Foster."

"Milk, eh?" responded Inspector Kirk, "and what is that supposed to mean? Are you talking about Ben Foster, the man who helped you in your little murder investigation last year?"

"It's not code," said Tenisha. "It's milk. We are only here because Lily left her handbag on Mr. Carlton's desk, and she needed her keys, her money, and the milk it could buy."

"A fortunate coincidence, wouldn't you say?"

"I'd say, but Detective Chasen's niece is not in the habit of arranging a murder," said Ted. "She's in the habit of seeing that the raison d'être of Mr. Singer's costumes for *The Ladder* are fully understood by the man who will review the play for *Variety*."

The EMS technicians closed the door to the ambulance.

"It doesn't look like he'll be in any condition to review a play tomorrow night," said the inspector as he ushered the women into the police car.

Kirk spent the time en route to the hospital asking questions. What did they ask the writer? What were they told? He stopped their responses only when the details of Singer's costumes were rushed upon him. He put a hand to his head and looked mournfully at the two women fate had, for the second year in a row, foisted upon him as he attempted to solve another case.

Suzie Sweet had been murdered, and he had two possible attempted murders to contend with, Mildred Trane's and Jimmy Carlton's, and all *Ladder* related. Except for the sirens, the police car was now silent. When it arrived at the hospital, Inspector Kirk wasted no time demanding information—about the patient's condition, prognosis, and ability to be questioned. Progress reports, he realized, he could get by telephone after dinner. All present were told the patient's prognosis was good, but when he would regain consciousness was unclear.

"I'll drive you home," the inspector told the women, "and I don't want you back here. If you're concerned about a man you met for an hour and a half, call me." He dropped Tenisha off first. At Lily's apartment, he rang Ben Foster's doorbell.

"Inspector Kirk, Mr. Foster. Remember me from last year? I'd like what you're holding for Miss Chasen."

Ben Foster looked puzzled. "Certainly, Inspector," and he produced a bottle of milk.

"Is that all, Mr. Foster?"

Ben Foster looked at Lily in dismay. "Don't tell me you've gotten involved in another murder case! What will your parents say?"

"My sentiment exactly," said Inspector Kirk, almost embracing his new comrade, as Lily, without a word, took the milk and climbed the stairs to her apartment.

Lily wanted to talk to Tenisha, but she worried that the police might have access to her telephone conversations. She also thought that Mildred Trane should know about the injury to her long-time friend, but should she be told the day before opening night? Probably not. After Carlton regained consciousness, it would be safe to inform his friend. Before that, she would only worry. Carlton's wife and children would be the first to see him. Were they aware of his friendship with Mildred Trane? If not, would Carlton want them to be? Certainly, Inspector Kirk wasn't aware of it. Well, she would wait until tomorrow at work, talk to Tenisha and together they would determine what to do next. Lily dialed the hospital and then Ted.

"I called the hospital. Jimmy Carlton just regained consciousness. Pick me up at 8:30 tomorrow morning. Visiting hours begin at nine. I'd like to see Carlton before Inspector Kirk does, and I know Carlton will be very happy to see you. He has bumps and bruises, but otherwise, he's in good shape. His wife and children are with him, hospital courtesy, but they can't take him home for at least another twenty-four hours, time to fully recover and be under observation."

"So, you think we can beat the inspector to Jimmy Carlton's bedside?"

"Probably, unless he takes business calls when he's off duty or has overheard this conversation."

Chapter Fifteen

"Thanks for the shove, Mr. Martin. I sure needed it!" The men shook hands. "I left your handbag in the hall safe, Miss Chasen. Glad you came back for it when you did!"

"Tenisha picked it up for me. Have you any idea what that hit- and-run was all about?"

"I'm threatened frequently, though not with a car until now. Honest reviewers lead dangerous lives."

"Do you think it could have anything to do with *The Ladder* or Mildred Trane?"

"Why should it? After opening night, maybe. It depends on what I write. And no, I won't be doing the bidding of the late Miss Suzie Sweet. My reviews are not meant to forward the aspirations of real-life players, even if 'all the world's a stage.'"

"You're familiar with the script."

"Absolutely, Miss Chasen. My column on the original *Ladder* was one of my finest devastating reviews. It's the changes that will make or break the play and determine my review."

"Have you ever seen a play that you enjoyed, but to which you gave a bad review?"

"Often, Ted. If the subject and the stars interest me, I know there's an excellent chance that I'll enjoy something about the performance. Most theatergoers are concerned about wasting their money or being on the wrong side of popularity. They wait for the reviews, and if they're bad, they do something else, play mahjong, see a baseball game, go dancing. If the reviews are generally good, they'll see the play and like it, whether they like it or not. There's so much to learn from life on the stage. We don't recognize ourselves, but we, our friends, our neighbors are there in some role or other. And if some plays are shallow, they reflect many lives off-stage. Edgar Davis has spent a small fortune trying to get that through to a thickheaded audience. I hope he's more successful in achieving his goal in this new production."

"Mrs. Trane liked the theme as well. Have you spoken to her about it?"

"Yes, Miss Chasen, but she knows what's good. No persuasion on my part was necessary or in order. I comment on things as requested. I don't lead people's lives for them."

"Pity your wife doesn't go with you to opening nights, or does she?"

"No, Miss Lily Ann Nosey Chasen. She hasn't even got as much as an autograph from Mildred Trane. I keep my home and business lives and acquaintances completely separate. Mrs. Carlton has, on occasion, seen Mildred Trane plays with her women friends. Mildred has told me that she has prevailed upon you to help her allay certain concerns. All these questions—could it be that you consider me a concern in her life?"

"You may unknowingly be aware of someone who is. That's what I'd like to find out."

"If I did, I would have told her."

"So, you've had no help to offer?"

"I hope I have, but it's for Mrs. Trane to tell you, not I." There was a knock on the door, but Inspector Kirk didn't wait for a response.

"You again—and again and again," he said with distaste.

"Inspector, if Miss Chasen were forty years old, instead of twenty-five, would you address her that way?"

Lily squeezed Jimmy Carlton's hand, smiled at Inspector Kirk, whose mouth had fallen open, and left, with Ted trotting behind.

Only two people were seated on a bench in the spot of green two blocks away from Singer Couture. They unwrapped their sandwiches and twisted open the bottles of juice.

"Remember last year, Ten, when were worried about someone poisoning our sandwiches?"

"I certainly do. We're in better shape today, maybe because we're not close enough to the murderer to matter to him or her." Vehicles whizzed by the vest-pocket enclave sheltering the young women. Tenisha pulled out a writing pad and placed it in Lily's lap as she bit into her tuna sandwich.

"License plate number, phone number and address. How did you manage that?"

"I dialed the Department of Motor Vehicles and had Donald demand the contact information for the driver who had sideswiped his car and damaged his fender. He was told they don't give out such information, to contact the police, so he pulled rank. He said he was a detective, and he gave his name and serial number."

"And they believed that fake story?"

"It wasn't all fake. They checked the serial number before they gave him the information."

"You made a one-in-a-million lucky guess, or are you psychic?"

"Neither, Lee. I gave them your Uncle Harry's name and number."

Lily put her head in her hands. Then, "All right. What's the driver's name."

"William Branten. Now, how do we go about questioning the Trane attorney?"

Chapter Sixteen

"I'm not a detective, I'm an attorney, Miss Chasen."

"I'm not asking you to be either, Mr. Branten. I just want to know where your Mercedes was yesterday afternoon at 3p.m."

"Aren't you a bit off the fashion track? The police haven't seen fit to question me like this."

"The police are not aware they should, but since Mr. Carlton and Mr. Martin, both friends of mine, were nearly killed by your vehicle, you can understand my personal interest in the whereabouts of your wheels."

"I'm sorry if my automobile caused you or your friends any distress, but I had nothing to do with it. I reported the theft of my vehicle to the police and the Department of Motor Vehicles. I've had a visit from the police with no mention whatever of its being involved in an accident."

"We did not share the license plate number of the hit-and-run vehicle with the police. Would you rather we had?"

"I have nothing to hide, but I am, of course, pleased that I have one less headache to contend with."

"You mean selection of the Trane you will represent in a divorce?"

"That and other things, Miss Chasen. Is Mrs. Trane aware you're in detective mode?"

"She's encouraged it. I know she's told you about her concern for her life."

"Yes, but I'm afraid her suspicion of being pushed down the stairs has escalated into a fear for her life wherever she goes. I value women's intuition greatly, but I'm afraid that hers has unduly affected her feelings about Mr. Trane and her marriage."

"Then you plan to represent Mr. Trane?"

"I didn't say that. Mr. Trane's behavior is reprehensible, but his family has been our firm's valued client since 1900. I will not allow personal feeling to enter into a professional decision."

"How, then, will you come to a professional decision?"

"Is it necessary for me to share that with you?"

"I would naturally like to know if I can trust you for information and trust you with information to help me assist her."

"I will consider the facts and attempt to come to a dispassionate decision."

"No, Mr. Branten, I'm not, as your look would indicate, a slip of a girl with no credentials for this task."

"I read about your work in the Lizette Frere murder case, and I was impressed. I can understand why Mrs. Trane would rather trust her fate to you than to the police, and I'm sure your uncle, Detective Harry Chasen, and your father, attorney Walter Chasen, have influenced your ability to solve mysteries."

"Did Mrs. Trane tell you about my uncle and my father?"

"No, just routine research in determining how to proceed in a case or potential case."

"Mr. Carlton and Mrs. Trane are long-time friends. Can you think of any reason someone would want to end that friendship?"

"A woman's dearest friend should be her husband, don't you think? Perhaps a competitor for her affections might resent their relationship. I'm in no way impugning Mrs. Trane's morals, but in examining the field of marital prospects, she may not be choosing wisely. There is some doubt as to whether her choice of Mr. Trane was a wise one. From my point of view, considering the benefit to him, it was a very wise one. I'm not taking sides, Miss Chasen. We live in an imperfect world, and people are imperfect."

"Are you willing to confide in me the results of the police efforts to determine who stole your Mercedes and why? You realize that if you do not, I shall have to inform the police that it was your vehicle that nearly collided with Mr. Carlton. I'm sure you agree that someone should."

"Someone should, naturally. I'll inform you of the results. Once I've determined the Trane I will represent, you will find me more affable or more businesslike, depending on whether I consider you a friend or an adversary. And now, if you'll excuse me, I have much to do. Goodbye, Miss Chasen."

"Goodbye, Mr. Branten. Will your decision be long in the making?"

"Who knows, Miss Chasen? I have a busy law firm. Never too busy for friends, of course, among which I number both Roland and Mildred Trane."

"Of course," echoed Lily, "of course."

Chapter Seventeen

"What am I, a delivery service? You don't want me picking up clothes the other models drop on the floor, you hired me as a model, you say. But it's all right for me to pick up and drop off clothes to this or that client. I've been doing a lot of that lately."

"Now Lee, only for a while longer. You're the only one I feel safe entrusting with my precious designs."

"What about Tenisha?"

"Yes, I trust her, but the clients don't know her well enough to trust her. Until the van is repaired, and my trained staff can resume deliveries, I can't take a chance of anyone in a taxi with my clothes but you, especially on a rainy day like this. You've only got three stops today, the last the most important. The stage entrance will be wet and muddy—the City of New York would decide to do sidewalk construction before the opening of an important play—so the cast will await their costumes at the front entrance."

Lily looked at the list. "I'm surprised the director didn't want the costumes for *The Ladder* before now."

"He didn't want them to get in the way of the tone, the dialogue and the relationships the actors were developing during rehearsals. The costumes are really for the audience. Ah, the taxi's at the curb. Let me help you with these."

Singer and Lily carefully placed the hangered garments in the taxicab. The boss handed Lily a wad of bills for her round-trip.

"I trust you," he repeated.

Lily smiled. Singer shut the door, and Lily and the clothes were off to various clients and their first theater rehearsal of a triumph in the making.

The Cort was a beautiful theatre, with red patterned carpet, elaborate carvings and crystal chandeliers. Producer Edgar Davis stood outside, beaming, as the taxicab ground to a halt. Behind him half a dozen anxious actors waited to claim their costumes, carefully carrying them through the elegant lobby and down and around the stage to their dressing rooms.

"Miss Chasen, please stay for a while. Every garment should fit well—heaven knows they've been tried on often enough, but just in case. I admit, I'd also like your opinion on the effect of the revision. I hear you saw it late last year."

"Yes, I'll be happy to stay." Lily banished the thought of Mrs. Winters, who was expecting to see her model the clothes Bernie had set aside for her.

The cast was ready. Mr. Davis clapped his hands and took an orchestra seat twelfth-row center next to director Murdock Pemberton. Bernard Singer's costumes turned the clock back to the year 1500 A.D. Lily was pleased with the effect, and it was obvious that Mr. Davis was, too. The tavern scene, even with minimal props, looked like something out of Shakespeare. The actors, with scripts in hand, did not alter the impression. Lily had refreshed her memory of the script by reading the copy Bernie had lent her. She felt no different than she did months before in the fall of 1927. Her interest was aroused, but would it last? Elements of foreboding and peace, of unease and calm descended upon the characters, who looked around in wonder, scanned the tavern rafters, spoke and desisted, as if spoken to by an unseen presence. Eerie music permeated the theatre at scene's end, and bolts of lightning and assorted brilliant colors saturated the ceiling and walls. Loudspeakers placed strategically throughout the theatre and the latest in visual technology saw to that. But even now, the actors seemed infused with unnatural knowledge that they were important, that what they were enacting meant something to them and to the universe. It was as if an invisible unearthly light were playing on them, waiting to burst forth and astonish those around them as well as themselves.

Lily thought, "The play's the thing in which to catch the conscience of the players." Shakespeare had said nothing about light and sound. Would an ethereal contagion move from players to audience? Would the new scenery add to the powerful effect? The lights flashed in concert with the dialogue, ebbing and flowing in colors muted and garish. In a mundane tavern, the dance of life, amazing movement in a relatively static, ordinary situation. Movement on the walls, the floor, the tables. Perhaps too much movement. The background music, though muted, was distracting, the never-ending play of light was distracting. Those in the drama seemed unaware of this. The producer and the director seemed unaware of this. Were they mesmerized by the dialogue, by the aural and visual setting? Lily rolled her eyes in disbelief and caught an unexpected movement. Surely the box that caught a flash of light was not meant to move, but suspended on a scaffold, it seemed to be inching forward. It was over the center of the stage. Now it was moving sideways, matching the movement of Mildred Trane. Did no one see? Mildred Trane moved in front of the scaffold and to its side. The box followed and began moving forward. Lily screamed, and Mildred Trane turned aside. The box landed at her feet in what sounded like a clap of thunder. Davis, Pemberton and the stagehands converged on the stage as Lily headed to the side exit. Barreling down the stairs from the loft was a figure in black. A gloved hand unlatched the door, and the figure dashed into the muddy street as Lily followed. She picked up a handful of caked mud from the construction site and threw a baseball pitch ahead of the fleeing figure, who disappeared around the corner. Lily hurried back inside.

"Mr. Davis, Mr. Pemberton, come quickly!"

She rushed them to a shoe print caught in the mud. "Don't move until the police get here!" Then she called Uncle Harry.

Davis and Pemberton had no intention of stopping the rehearsal for an "accident," so they parked Lily with an umbrella by the footprint in the cool April air while they continued the rehearsal with the shaken but "game" actors. Ten minutes later, Detective Harry Chasen arrived with Inspector Kirk and a footprint expert.

"Man's shoes, size 11," said Chasen, as the inspector questioned the actors and stage crew. Harry Chasen lifted the metal box onto a nearby table. "Whew! It's heavy. All steel. Could have crushed the skull of anyone beneath it." He opened the box. "Rocks." He turned a few over in his hands. "Like the rocks on the beach at Newport. Not local rocks, for sure. Mr. Pemberton, why the scaffold and why the box?"

"Scaffold for painting backdrops. It should already have been removed. Box for paint."

"Where's the paint?"

"Should be in the closet."

Lily followed her uncle upstairs. He looked in the closet. On the floor were paint cans surrounded by a circle of rocks. "Too many to fit in the box," he said. "But how did Mr. Size 11 shoes get these huge rocks up here?" He looked around. "Freight elevator. He certainly wasn't taking any chances. Even without the rocks, the box could have destroyed the person underneath."

"Do you think he had an in-house collaborator, Uncle Harry?"

"He had to have detailed knowledge about staging and the director's orders about movement and the layout of this theater from someone, but who and why?" Harry Chasen poked around the walls, floors, table and empty closet. "Let's see what the inspector has come up with." Chasen and his niece descended the stairs.

Lily stopped. "Uncle Harry." She stamped on a stair board near the railing.

He stopped, sat on a stair, and ran a hand under it. He moved down a few stairs, pulled out a flashlight and looked at the stair above. "This board is loose. And rotten. And newly installed. Someone's installed a rotten stair board."

Inspector Kirk approached Chasen and Lily. "Find anything, Harry?"

"No, sir," Chasen said loudly. He looked at Lily. "Maybe," he said softly. Edgar Davis was approaching.

"This is terrible," moaned Davis. "Who would do such a thing? We're all devoted to this production."

"Do any of the crew go up to the loft during the course of the play?"

"A few, yes, but as I told you, Inspector Kirk, there was no need for that today. All the stairs bothered me at first, but they're in excellent condition. Everyone can manage them, even Mildred, despite the twisted ankle she received recently slipping on a banana peel outside Singer Couture." He eyed Lily reproachfully. "She can hold onto the railing. She insists it won't be a problem. Roland's idea, you know. Double-decker stage creates interest, allows more to go on, more for the eye to feast on."

Inspector Kirk turned to Lily. "Miss Chasen, there's nothing further to keep you here; you've delivered the costumes. Shouldn't you be getting back to your day job?"

Lily kissed Uncle Harry on the cheek and left. She heard Inspector Kirk's parting shot.

"So unprofessional, these amateur detectives!"

Chapter Eighteen

Mildred Trane was escorted to her table by Bernard Singer. Heads turned, as he knew they would. Singer signaled for the weekly showing to begin. As the lights dimmed, Fred, an attendant, escorted a lone woman in an outlandish hat to a table near the side door. She veered off and headed straight for Mildred Trane, who jumped up immediately before sitting down again with the new- comer. They spoke briefly before turning their attention to the stage and the first model starting down the runway. Fred arrived at the designated table, scratched his head, bewildered, and exited through the side door. There was, in time, a brief respite for the audience to digest what it had seen.

"It was daring of you to wear my wings to the theater last week. More wings for you, my dear, both literal and figurative. Was Bernie upset with you?"

"He didn't show it."

"Very wise. But he was more attentive, more solicitous of your wishes, wasn't he?"

"Yes, how did you know?"

"We're all that way. Designer psychology. Patronizing another house has dual benefits: a new look for the woman, a new appreciation of her by her usual designer. Worth considering."

Lily was now modeling a suit.

"No hips," said the newcomer. "Could be a disaster, but not the way she moves in it. Clothing is not meant to do all the work."

Tenisha Jones strode strongly onto the stage. The newcomer turned to Mildred Trane. "This is why I've come, my dear, to see how

Miss Jones performs. Very well! I've come to steal her, not you." Her eyes quickly scanned the room until they alighted on the apoplectic gaze of Bernard Singer. "I've been discovered." She turned back to Mildred Trane and whispered, "Don't turn red and don't apologize—ever!" Her eyes met the coffee and tea pots on the table. "Only in America or England. Viva la France!" The unexpected guest remained quiet for the duration of the showing.

When the lights came on, patrons and guests murmured discreetly, and motioned to attendants for encore viewings of specific garments. Bernard Singer slowly made his way to Trane and company, smiling, chatting briefly with familiar and potential clients, many in for a week of New York shopping, which is why Singer held weekly showings of his season's clothes, varying them from week to week. Stoutly facing Mildred Trane, he kissed her on the cheek and bowed to the uninvited guest.

"It is an honor," he said grandly.

Elsa Schiaparelli nodded her agreement. "I don't do this for everyone. I see you are still up to your fashionable tricks on an elegant palette. Bravo!"

"Thank you, Madame Schiaparelli. We are both masters of tricks."

"Come, come, Bernie. We are not enemies. Address me as a fellow trickster devoted to the art."

"All right, Schiap. You certainly have the better of me in your sources. What inspirations have Dali and Picasso provided for your fall collections?"

"Too soon to reveal, Bernie. I note you are not revealing yours. You are undoubtedly continuing your liaison with Walter Martin Fabrics. It would be foolish to stop, but you are safe. I will not try to entice Mr. Martin with a more lucrative deal. I'm not sure I could. Anyway, we Europeans stick together. And why not, with so many appealing fabric designers from which to choose? How is your dark model working out?"

"Very well. Our clients appreciate her."

"Very daring, very Schiaparelli!"

Singer turned pale.

"But you can Schiap-up your collection without her. May I illustrate?" Before Singer could respond, she walked to the apron of the runway with a travel case and unlatched it. Out onto the runway tumbled a colorful array of scarves. The models showing Singer's wares at various tables turned to look, as did Singer's patrons.

"With music!" Schiap proclaimed boldly. "Miss Chasen need not sing. She can watch and learn."

Bernard Singer's face was beginning to burn. A new performance was about to begin. A few notes into Sue's piano playing, he reached the stage. "Ladies and gentlemen," he announced, "I am pleased to present Madame Elsa Schiaparelli, queen of avant-garde design."

"Friends," she began, "Mr. Singer has allowed me to demonstrate accessory magic to transform your Bernard Singer purchases into new creations. You can enjoy two outfits for the price of one, and marry both refinement and daring, to the amazement, even envy, of your friends." She motioned for the first model to walk down the runway. Lily did so. "Ladies, here is a lovely conservative linen suit with a low waist. Attach streamers to it (she held up dressmaker tape and several scarves), and change it at will, from solid colors to patterns, from familiar to strange. Let your imagination fly with the streamers, let the straight skirt dance with movement and color. Bring it alive as your hips turn. Too tall already, and no need for vertical stripes? Try a scarf at the waist for horizontal flair. Be as daring or conservative as you wish. But now, the choice is yours, not the designer's. Even more horizontally inclined?" Schiap motioned for Margo to step forward. "Try bands around your arms, your waist. The same design will give the illusion of strength, of confidence. The simple dress becomes an emblem of success, the bands of war culminating in victory."

"Simple dress," muttered Bernard Singer. "The finest peau de soie shimmers with femininity. The war is over."

But Schiap charged on. "Ah, the feminine grace of the skirt. Join to it the flowers of this oversized handkerchief at the bosom, pouring like a waterfall from the pocket of the blouse, with a floral pin created just so on the other side. So much magic from Mr. Singer's elegant basics." Bernard Singer was about to explode.

"Now, the elegant lady as the little woman in the kitchen, though she isn't quite sure where it is in the house." Jenny appeared on the stage. "Curled and crimped scarves change the straight skirt into an exotic apron, like so, and an improvised apron collar mimics it in the back. Charming and feminine, coming or going. Scarves in all shapes, sizes and colors await your personal touch. Available from most designers, Schiaparelli scarves, of course, being distinctive, as she herself is reputed to be. Think of what you can do!"

"I am," muttered Bernard Singer, as his eye fell upon a loose rope coiled near the stage.

Excited women left their tables and converged on Madame Schiaparelli. The models left the runway for the dressing room, but a raised Schiaparelli finger detained Tenisha and Lily, motioning them to the table the designer had recently vacated, where Mildred Trane still sat. Fifteen minutes later, the designer joined them.

"My dear Miss Jones, I reiterate my offer with enthusiasm. You need not answer now." She glanced at Bernard Singer bidding effusive farewells to his guests. "I feel I owe my clients the best I have to offer and, Mildred Trane, what I have to offer you, if what I've heard sotto voce is correct, is information you may find useful. Rumors abound, dear Mildred, and if they are to any degree true, your lawyer's past adventures may interest you. The murder of Miss Suzie Sweet does complicate your predicament, even perhaps endangers you, as you probe for a satisfactory conclusion. I've found that husbands are not indispensable. Disposability is not a one-way street, but perhaps that is just me.

"You should know that a year before your husband made Miss Sweet's acquaintance, she was in an intimate relationship with your attorney, William Branten. I have found that when a man spends a large sum on a woman's wardrobe, notice I did not say 'lady,' he expects more than a thank-you. They visited my salon in Paris. She returned twice during the week for fittings. She chose ensembles that were Schiaparelli with touches of Bernard Singer. I must satisfy conservatives too, you know. Too avant-garde a look for her solemn boyfriend would not have been appropriate. Price was no object, somewhat surprising, since I heard he had lost a great deal the previous week at the tables in Monte Carlo. Retaining such a man to profitably extricate you from your dilemma might bear rethinking."

"I'm hoping not to retain his services at all, Schiap, but should I be unable to hold my husband, Mr. Branten may not be an available attorney. He has declined to state which of us he would represent if our marriage dissolves."

"Where does his profit lie? Apparently, he hasn't determined that yet. Suzie Sweet is replaceable, you less so, but there are no guarantees. I just thought that you, dear Mildred, and your team should be aware that your legal executor did to his wife what your husband has done to you. You may draw your own conclusion as to where his sympathy lies. Where his profit lies may, of course, nullify the effects of his sympathy." She rose. "My offer to you, Miss Jones, remains, to take effect after you and Miss Chasen have helped extricate Mrs. Trane from her dilemma, which may intensify into a charge of murder. I could stand your hair on end with stories of where our police have gone awry, but you young ladies had a bucketful of that last year. I was an avid follower of your successful adventure. I wish you all well. Do consider looking on the Schiap side of things, Mildred. At first glance, it may seem outlandish, but it's practical. Believe me, in my lifetime I've seen it all."

"Avoid Bernie if you can, Lee. He's not in a good humor." Tenisha folded the newspaper and smacked a three-column headline in "The Arts" section:

*　　*　　*

ELSA SCHIAPARELLI INVADES BERNARD SINGER COUTURE. WILL SINGER TEAM UP WITH HER?

"It makes Bernie seem desperate," sighed Tenisha. "Notice who initiates the liaison. Reporters have their own bias, but you'd think it would be an American, not a French/Italian one."

"It does have a ring of truth. Our store ads keep bowing to European style. But let's get back to our charge, Mildred Trane. Three years ago, the late Miss Sweet was a Schiap girl. Her last fashion effort was to become a Davenport girl. Flexible, adaptable. All to meet her man's perceived needs. Is Branten as flexible about his clients, Ten?"

"Why should it matter, Lee? There are other outstanding attorneys. Anyway, that's beyond our realm. In the murder category, he's an outside force."

"He was at the door when Roland nearly tumbled from the library ladder. He was near when Mildred felt pushed at the top of the stairs." Lily frowned.

"How could he be in two places at once, Lee? Either he was knocking on the front door, or he was in the house. For that matter, how could Roland have had the ladder pushed from under him in the ground floor library and then have been at the top of the stairs in the center hall pushing his wife as she and Inspector Kirk seem to think possible? The house staff--?"

"Who have been with the Tranes forever."

"As has William Banten."

"We're missing something here."

"Lunch," said Tenisha. "Let's go."

Chapter Nineteen

The lights were blazing in the lobby of the Cort Theatre, and so many individuals huddled together in groups that it was difficult for singletons to maneuver past them to the bar or to the table heaped high with nightshirts and posters featuring the name of Mildred Trane in the boldest of type and a humongous ladder. An electric buzz was in the air, with only "Mildred, Mildred Trane" clearly audible. The old *Ladder* had lapsed two weeks earlier, and its replacement would begin within the hour. The lobby was not used to this—the crowds, the tuxedos, the animated faces, the Chanels, Schiaparellis, Poirets, Boulangers that punctuated the floor. Who was looking, who was counting, who was aware? For once, not the theatergoers, who were preoccupied with this history-making event. Would Mildred Trane be a Joan of Arc, who would be warmly remembered as the heroine who had salvaged the unsalvageable, or an actress who foolishly destroyed the reputation she had so carefully nurtured over fifteen years? And *The Ladder*, what of *The Ladder*, which her husband had made his? Theatergoers felt free to voice their opinions while awaiting the debut of the resurrected drama.

"Roland can't act. What makes him think he can write?"

"Mildred's a devoted wife, but devoted to the point of suicide?" The speaker shook his head.

"Mildred can work miracles."

"When has she worked miracles? She's carefully chosen outstanding plays. Miracles weren't necessary."

"Maybe we're underestimating Roland."

"Maybe tortoises can fly."

"Get a grip, gentlemen. We're here to see a play, *The Ladder*." The female voice was firm.

"No, darling. The reviewers are here to see *The Ladder*. We're here to see Mildred Trane, and by extension Roland Trane, and what we say when we leave this theater will spread like wildfire, will trump the reviewers, whatever they say. It may not be fair, but it's life. Pray for Mildred, darling."

Lily Chasen waved to Tenisha Jones who, her hand in Donald's, was slowly moving through the crowd to join Lee and Ted. The glow of youthful expectation was in their eyes.

"This is a good omen," said Ten, looking at the masses who carpeted the floor. Lily, who had overheard some of the comments, smiled wanly.

"There's Bernie in the corner, talking to Ted's dad, Lee. 'Birds of a feather.'"

Lily laughed. "Look!" She pointed to Singer, now speaking to a woman wearing Chanel. "Polite and restrained. Look again at the volubility, exuberance and charm of which he's so beautifully capable when addressing a woman wearing a Singer!"

Tenisha scanned the lobby. "No Jimmy Carlton, but no John LeRoy, either. Isn't he Carlton's usual substitute?"

"Yes, but maybe Carlton insisted on doing an opening night review a day or two after opening night."

"Would *Variety* allow him to do that?"

"Look—there's William Branten, Ten, alone."

"If Carlton doesn't bring his wife to opening nights, maybe Branten doesn't either. To them, a premiere is business. Well, shall we go to our seats?"

"Do you mind, Lily, if Tenisha and I stay here a bit longer?" asked Donald. "The architecture of theaters has always fascinated me."

"Me, too," said Tenisha without enthusiasm.

"Why are gold carvings so traditional in theaters?" mused Donald.

"Because they enhance the stage experience, and even make up for it to some degree if it is lacking. The old world has aways been a glamorous and stable world, in retrospect." The voice turned to Lily. "Do you remember me?" Willie Simpson bowed and kissed Lily's hand.

Lily introduced Tenisha, Donald and Ted. Ted's "Are you someone we should know?" took Lily by surprise.

"I'm delighted to meet you all, even *you*," Willie hurled at Ted, his wink at Lily not escaping anyone.

"I'm delighted to meet you," enthused Donald, explaining why, while Ted eyed the building and architecture whiz suspiciously.

"This promises to be a landmark evening," said an excited Willie.

"Landmarks can come crashing down," said a voice in the crowd that hurried past.

"Nothing and no one can destroy Mildred Trane," said Willie firmly.

Lily and Tenisha looked at each other solemnly. Did this opening night have nothing at all to do with the play?

*   *   *

While the men were talking baseball in their seats, Tenisha and Lily looked around the lavish theater. Roland's mother and sister were sixth-row center. Willie was two rows behind them, and a few rows from the rear was William Branten.

"No Inspector Kirk," said Tenisha.

"Foolish man. So many suspects are gathered under one roof. And more than that." Lily pointed fifth-row center, where a somewhat battered Jimmy Carlton sat stoically awaiting the curtain's rise. "We have two intermissions to work with, Ten. I think the answers to some of our questions lie in the past. I think it's more than the challenge of the theme that attracted Mildred Trane to it. I think it's fiction metamorphosing in real time, in real lives, hers and Roland's."

"It would help if they were speaking to each other."

"They will in time, Ten, and certainly in the play. I recall one reviewer who said he came often to *The Ladder* for the peace and quiet in the near-empty theater, for relaxation. I couldn't understand that, because when Ted and I saw it, we were struck by its moral indictment of society. It's a morality play, a medieval morality play that has moved beyond its time. Billed as such, it could have had a niche following."

"Hardly enough, Lee, to give it a substantial Broadway run."

"True, but it may have had enough of a run to affect the audience and the play's participants, which is probably why Mildred Trane has dared to act in it. That's what the murmurings in the lobby were about—that regardless of what the reviewers say, tonight is about Mildred and Roland Trane. Scary to think you're putting yourself up for review by the world." Lily's eyes scanned the balcony, the walls, the ceiling's elaborate decor. "No falling surprises that I can see. I expect the only surprises will be onstage. Too bad that muddy shoeprint wasn't enough to determine Mildred Trane's would-be assassin." The theater darkened, and a slumping Jimmy Carlton sat bolt upright. Lily and Tenisha sat back in their seats, and their baseball-addict dates turned their attention to the stage. Lily pulled out a small notebook and a pen.

"So, your business school training and experience at Walter Martin Fabrics hasn't gone to waste."

Lily smiled at her friend. "Curtain going up!"

*   *   *

It was intermission. Ted and Donald were getting the wine and pastry, and Lily and Tenisha moved to the relative calm at the foot of the staircase to the balcony. The lobby was alive with small talk, but faces were alert and interested in what lay ahead. 1679 lay ahead.

"From 1300 to 1549 was quite a leap, but the machinery Roland used to show character connections was awesome—that release from body and costume in 1300 and a drop into new ones in 1549! However did he do it? And what an amazing use of slides and walls, of light and shadows."

Ten shivered. "And frightening, too, Lee! Was Sir Philip Clifford's suicide necessary, I wonder? After all, he is scarred and fettered and made a slave, though to a goodhearted mercer, 250 years later."

"Mildred Trane insisted. She said that two hundred and fifty years of escape from punishment for colluding with his beloved Margaret in the murder of her husband was too long a wait for justice."

"She was a very convincing Lady Margaret, Lee, and Sir Philip's cowardice in blaming her for bewitching him in an age when witchcraft was taken seriously was a reprehensible thing to do. I wish the scene had been continued. Was Lady Margaret Percy truly burned at the stake, or did her appeal to the king spare her life? As the Act II wife of the innkeeper, who treats her like a slave, she gets punished for eliminating her husband in Act I. Of course, we can't be sure she killed him, perhaps her boyfriend did, but the evidence, though circumstantial, is strong that she either did it or conspired with him to do it or have it done."

"A triangle, as in the Trane's real lives, Ten. Mildred insisted that Sir Philip's punishment be self-inflicted, because then he recognizes he has done wrong. Do you think Roland recognizes that he has wronged Mildred?"

"And perhaps seen to it that Suzie Sweet is murdered to make amends? She was the last chorus girl off the stage, Lee, an easy mark for even a novice well-positioned in the audience."

"But why kill her, why not just drop her, pay her off, why something so deadly?'

"She could talk, give lurid accounts of their escapade, shame Mildred Trane."

Lily nodded. "Or someone else might fear lurid stories from her. She was William Branten's mistress for a while. She could make Roland look like a fool. Roland and Mildred both had reasons to keep her permanently silent."

"Do you think, Lee, that Mildred's fear for her life is a sham, that we and Bernie are being used to deflect suspicion away from her and a well-planned elimination of Suzie Sweet?"

"She's an actress, not a playwright, Ten, but she might be trying her hand at a script."

"Look, our little oasis is about to increase by two."

The woman who was both mother and mother-in-law of the parties under discussion was descending upon them, led by a young addition. The ladies moved back to allow the newcomers space without blocking the staircase, but the younger woman with a longer stride than her companion moved ahead of her, holding her hand and steering her toward Lily and Tenisha.

"Hello," she said brightly. "You must remember me. From Small's Paradise," she added.

"We remember," chorused the models.

"How could you forget? I was at the center of a one-act play, rather like *The Ladder*, with no real conclusion to it. I'm Vivian Trane." She laughed. "So you know why I'm here, though I would have come anyway. Mildred Trane is one of my great favorites. I was privileged to see her two years ago in London, my birthday treat, and I've been dying to meet her. And this is my mother, Elizabeth Trane." There were smiles and nodded greetings, as Mrs. Trane looked with admiration and exasperation at her daughter.

"We expected you to be more of a mouse," said Lily.

"Would that she were," murmured her mother.

Vivian laughed. "I keep telling Mama that's not very wise, given the world we're in. I kept telling the nuns that, too. I suppose I now have to explain about the nuns," she said ruefully.

"We know about the nuns."

"Do you? Good! But how—"

"I've met your protective brother, though only once, and Ten and I know your sister-in-law. I'm Lily Chasen, and my friend is Tenisha Jones. We are both models at Bernard Singer Couture, Mildred Trane's favorite couturier."

Vivian clapped her hands in childish glee. "How wonderful! I haven't been in this country since I was one year old. In fact, I've never met my sister-in-law."

"Vivian—" Her mother's voice had a warning in it.

"Too late to silence me, darling." She patted her mother's hand. "There can't be any secrets where Row is concerned. He's too famous, too rich, too important. I read the American newspapers," she explained. "Living in Nowhere-Land, it's the only way to keep informed. I'm very sad about Row and Mildred, but I may have changed his mind the night you saw us. At least I hope so. I intend to keep trying, and we're not going home until I succeed. By the time some newspaper gets the old, degrading story, there will be a new, happier one to contradict it." Mama's expression brightened. "I don't expect you know Mildred personally."

"We do. We would do anything to help her."

"But not Roland?"

"Mildred Trane does not want to divorce your brother," said Lily.

"Oh, then you do want to help him. That horrid woman is all wrong for him."

"He won't be marrying her," said Tenisha. Elizabeth Trane now gave Tenisha a warning look.

"What a relief," said Vivian.

"Not much you could do if he had done so." Added Tenisha

"I'd be very tempted to kill her," laughed Vivian. "I'm not an ordinary Mildred Trane fan.

"Darling, let's return to our seats. You know how slowly I walk these days."

Vivian Trane patted her mother's hand again but ignored her request. "Something's wrong, something the newspapers don't know yet. What is it?"

"Darling—"

"Hush, Mama."

Tenisha and Lily looked at each other, then Lily spoke. "Miss Suzie Sweet died suddenly late last week."

Vivian Trane turned pale. "You mean she was murdered." The ensuing silence was her answer. "And you think Roland did it because she was unkind to me, or Mildred did it, because she was wrong for Roland."

"For a young lady living in opulent, secluded isolation, you're very perceptive. Only it's not what we think, it's what the police are considering," said Lily.

Vivian's pale smile coincided with a bell resounding through the theater. She held out her hands to Lily and Tenisha. "We'll meet again," she said as she and her mother turned away. The models were two of the last to their seats before the theater darkened. As they passed Jimmy Carlton on the aisle, Lily glanced at the pad in his lap. She read, "Great as usual, but the play???"

"I'm enjoying it, Ten. Why do reviewers find it so hard to like?"

"We've seen two acts that aren't related, each one incomplete. Oh, in time, there will be a relationship, but people aren't patient. They don't want their endings 'in time.' They don't want to have to think: What are the ramifications of what has happened in each act? As I recall, even by play's end, we don't know. We merely get the general message that everything has been leading up to—that our past affects our future. People go to plays for entertainment, not messages. They don't want messages, or advice or answers."

"But we do, Ten." She turned her head toward Vivian and Elizabeth Trane. "Wild cards, but very worth pursuing."

The curtain rose on a London gambling house. It was 1867.

*   *   *

While Donald waved toward this or that part of the ceiling or walls, explaining to an attentive Ted some architectural formation or historical trend, Lily and Tenisha sipped tea at a tiny, round table in the corner of the lobby.

"Another triangle, Lee. The newly minted Duke of Haverlea falls for the lies of a country bumpkin about the infidelity of his mistress, which mistress said bumpkin hopes to replace."

"And murder is the result. The mistresses keep changing. Their men, married or unmarried, keep them for a while. Then boredom or lies set in, and they're gone. Roland didn't change that. This script is something he understands, Ten. And the wives put up with it, like Lady Lisle, who gets a consolation gift when she confronts her husband."

"And meanwhile she's having a passionate affair of her own!"

"Mildred Trane has put up with it, but she's had no affairs of her own."

"That we know of, Lee. Hardly Mr. Engineer. Maybe Willie. Jimmy Carlton is a possibility. Why else would he come tonight in his condition?"

"He could rightly believe that a good friend's printed judgment would be important to Mildred. But if Mildred Trane had or has lovers, they could opt for murder of her husband's latest mistress for making her life miserable and unhinging her marriage. As *The Ladder* clearly indicates, lovers do not necessarily want their mistresses' marriages unhinged, especially if they are married themselves."

"Yes, indeed, Lee. They could then be in line to succeed Roland, not necessarily an appealing prospect if they prefer to maintain their freedom with intimacy on the side. Like Willie, if he were her lover."

"Or the prim and proper Robert Blair, who sanctifies conservatism and order. And while Jimmy Carlton is a family man, he might be a family-and-a-half man." Lily sighed.

"Well, look at that! Jimmy Carlton talking to William Branten. If only we were nearby! Oh, that won't be necessary." Hovering at the men's side was Vivian Trane, nursing a drink. She lingered for a moment or two, then elbowed her way diligently through the crowd to the far side of the lobby, where Willie, the building writer, and Robert, the building engineer, were engrossed in conversation.

"That's no coincidence," affirmed Lee. "The men are taking no notice of her at all. They don't know her. She's done her research! But where's the matriarch? Ah, there she is, coming slowly down the stairs. Vivian Trane has made good use of her mother's visit to the powder room. A confining and secluded upbringing hasn't dampened her spirit one bit. And she certainly is a woman of spirit!"

"And determination, Lee. They're staying at the Roosevelt Hotel. Why not the Trane mansion, I wonder?"

"Vivian hasn't met Mildred Trane yet, and Mildred is dropping by the showroom tomorrow afternoon to try on a dress Molly altered before the Singer show. It would be an appropriate time for the women to meet."

"So we override the meeting Roland may have planned?"

"I think that's best, Ten. She's heard from Roland, certainly at Small's. Now it's time for her to meet her sister-in-law without his presence. I'm pretty certain her mother would concur. There's the bell. Act IV, New York City, 1840. No leering, murderous intent as I recall, only a bunch of female gossips ranged against the son of a wealthy political figure, intent on marrying a performer who doesn't wear much onstage. Shades of Suzie Sweet! And then Roland catapults us into Act V, in modern times, in an unnamed great American city, where a young man on the verge of marriage wants to give away millions to start a foundation to help the poor help themselves. He won't be bankrupt, but his father thinks he's nuts."

"Tons of people think Edgar Davis is nuts, Lee, for pouring a fortune into *The Ladder* with a message to reform society. Acts IV and V may be an anticlimax after the philandering, murderous hijinks we've seen in the first three acts."

"Time will tell. I'd guess an hour, and then we're off to an early breakfast and music and skating waiters at Small's Paradise. I'm starved!"

Chapter Twenty

Everything was at a standstill at Singer Couture. Newspapers were flying all over the place. Bernard Singer had ordered all the models to read the reviews of his coming out on the Broadway stage. There would be no morning clients. Mildred Trane would be the first arrival at noon, and the runway show would commence at one o'clock. The Singer models shouted out printed comments while Singer beamed: "Stunning costumes, better than the lines deserved," "color and shimmer where needed most," "costumes a perfect reflection of each era," and best of all, "Singer is a master of both simplicity and elegance."

"Our advertising agency will be in heaven!" exclaimed Singer, who was already there, "but will the play last? Great costumes for a failed play --" He shook his head.

"Picture this," said Lily, a newspaper held high in her hands, her eyes closed: "A decent run. The play only lasted this long because of Bernard Singer!"

Singer looked eagerly at Lily, frowning as he held up a review.

"*The Ladder* has a four-month advance booking, thanks to Mildred Trane fans," Lily assured him.

Singer brightened. "That's true, Lee, and it wasn't all that bad. If there weren't unfinished episodes meant to tantalize the audience, it would have been quite good, especially at the beginning, not just because of my costumes, but because there was skulduggery in the plot."

"It was pretty tame toward the end," piped up Sally.

"Now, now, writing a play is difficult, and I would imagine that rewriting one, especially one you haven't written, is even more so. Mildred Trane's husband did a fine job." Singer's head gave a decisive, affirmative nod, and all the models, who had been given balcony seats and binoculars, nodded likewise.

When play review perusals had ended, the models were set to work clipping them and highlighting in yellow all mention of Bernard Singer's contribution to the performance. Fortunately, all mention of him was favorable, and the busy, often anxious atmosphere at his House only crept into evidence as the noon hour approached. The fitting room Mildred Trane would soon enter was bedecked with an assortment of flowers suitable in variety and quantity to the Botanical Garden, and the red carpet for her extended from the Singer entrance through the dressing room.

Mildred Trane arrived to much acclaim and cheers and was sequestered in her dressing room for the next half hour, after which she was feted in his office by *The Ladder's* costume designer, from whence could be heard peals of laughter and the rustling of newspapers. Vivian Trane arrived at 12:45 and was ushered into Singer's office by Lily, who left the boss making awkward introductions to the two women. He joined Lily a few minutes later, mopping his brow. "Such excitement!" And he ordered all the models into the dressing room to prepare for the weekly show that was only fifteen minutes away. Lily sang two dresses onto the runway, Sue, proficient as usual at the piano, before Pierre's attractive nasal voice took over and Lily started down the runway in a smart suit with an art-deco-spangled jacket. Half the vocal accompaniment in the show would be hers, the rest Pierre's, the young Frenchman unable to shake the sadness that still crept into his voice from time to time. He missed his compatriot Lizette, the model who had been murdered the year before. Lily, too, was often preoccupied, but it didn't show. She still reveled in the beautiful clothes she modeled that she could not afford to buy, but more and more, her thoughts turned to her dream, to the music career that could not escalate until she started it, and that would not happen without additional training, preferably from a prominent teacher whose recommendation would persuade a small vocal society or opera group to take her on, for a trial at least. She would have to continue modeling for a while, though singing in cabarets was still an option, if she could survive on the pay. She insisted on at least having bread on the table. Of course—she looked down at the stunning suit she was modeling—the luxury she lived in from 9 to 5 here or at accessory houses was not distasteful, and the audience paid attention, not always the case in a cabaret, as they ate their supper and drank their wine. Tenisha ended the show with a stunning Georgian print dress that fell below the knee. Now guests were requesting another look at some of the pieces. Lily could not leave yet. Vivian and Mildred Trane, who took their seats as the lights dimmed to avoid attention from the clients who were fashion-bent, were talking avidly and amicably at a table in the corner. As Lily turned front and back for two clients interested in her broad-collared dress with a wide inverted pleated skirt, she saw Joseph deliver an envelope to the Trane table. Vivian Trane opened it, put her hand to her mouth, and passed it to Mildred, who read it, instantly stood up, and with her arm through Vivian's, quickly left the room. Lily was finished. She motioned to Tenisha, who was twirling one final time for a client, and they both hurried after the Tranes, who were heading toward Singer's office. They turned the corner to see a puzzled Singer addressing the pair as the door slammed shut. Lily hurried to change while Tenisha stood guard and then Lily did likewise. They waited a respectable distance from the office, until ten minutes later, the door opened, and a blanch-faced trio exited.

Lily and Tenisha approached them. "May we help?" Both women gripped the models' hands, while Singer looked solemn. "We want to help," echoed Tenisha. The group headed to the lounge, which Singer emptied with a sweep of his hand. Vivian handed the letter to Lily and Tenisha who, heads together, read it in silence:

Dear Vivian,

I love you very much. You are in my heart, but I must go. I haven't made much of an imprint in this life—many starts, few substantial middles, and no lasting conclusions. The Trane & Co. success story is not mine. Others have done wonders in my name. My periodic attempts at acting have come to naught, and my playwriting skills have been questioned by reviewers I respect.

I deserve no credit for the success of my marriage, such as it's been. I don't seem to have the knack for living a successful and happy life. I've decided to try again in another realm. A fresh start is what I need. You are well provided for; I've left new instructions with Branten. My darling sister, I wish you a blessed life. I think you'll get it too, because you'll know how to handle it. I'll be fine.

Don't waste a minute mourning for me. That's an order! I love you and always will. You're in my heart forever!

Until we meet again,
Roland

"We called his office, and he hasn't been there all day. We called the house, and Roderick checked his closets. All his clothes are gone. His Lincoln is still in the driveway. We called the train station and the airlines. No one with his name or description bought a ticket to anywhere this morning. It had to be this morning. There were no reviews until this morning. We're afraid to think what this means." Mildred Trane's face was white.

"Don't worry in advance," said Tenisha.

Joseph stuck his head past the lounge door. "Pardon me, but a Roderick just called for Mrs. Trane. He said he found a letter on her bed from Mr. Trane."

"Bernie, ladies, we must leave. I'll call you from home."

"You'll have our complete support. Whatever we can do..." Singer trailed off.

* * *

"Amazing, isn't it?" Lily sipped her soda in their favorite little park mere blocks from Singer Couture. "If everyone who fluffed it in life committed suicide, we'd have a very empty planet."

"He took his clothes with him. I don't think they're necessary on the other side."

"At least he knew he wasn't a great husband, Ten, and knew what his talents were not, but running away without having solved his problems guarantees he'll repeat them. What's the point? You can't run away from yourself."

"Apparently Roland thinks he can—a new look, a new identity, not a deep enough change, but a start. At least he was thoughtful of his understudy and wished him well, and of Mildred, too. He didn't try to change his will or prenup. Most of his fortune still goes to her."

"I think she would have preferred him. And Vivian gets the company. What does a slip of a girl know about running an enterprise like Trane & Co.?"

"Not much, Lee. She doesn't even know about cosmetics. Except for lipstick, she doesn't use any. What a great complexion! But the executives that made Roland look good will train her well. I think, though, that she'll end up being the company leader. She's not a you-do-it-I'll-take-the-credit kind of girl. But his mother, poor woman, she took it hard. That beautiful letter he left her can't be much solace. She's lost her son. Well, it looks like our part in the Mildred Trane Mystery is over. The two prime suspects are dead. The attempt on the life of Mildred's maid, the missing then returned green bracelet, the falling box of rocks that could have taken her life during theater rehearsals, Roland could have easily done them all."

"Could have, Ten, but did he? Mildred could have imagined an attempt to push her down the stairs, and Roland was probably responsible for the bracelet incident, but I can't be easy in my mind that Roland did the other things and that Mildred is safe to carry on her life without fear. Roland didn't confess to murderous designs in any of his letters. And what of the attempted murder of Jimmy Carlton?"

"If Roland was disenchanted with Suzie Sweet because of her behavior toward his sister, he may have decided against divorce and felt that Carlton's close relationship with his wife threatened to undo his marriage."

"After all these years, Ten? Roland's letters don't supply sufficient closure to this case. The police are implying that they do, the living parties involved are willing, even eager to accept that they do, but they don't. I don't want assumptions as to what happened; I want answers. Messy and displeasing though they may be, answers are what we need. Uncle Harry says there's a nationwide search on for Roland Trane. None of his letters uses the word 'suicide,' and he did take his clothes with him."

"Vivian and Mildred can't probate the will until the coroner issues a death certificate, but the wait is bringing two women, really three, closer together. That's good, at least."

"Mother Trane shares cash and the proceeds of Roland's investments with her daughter, as well as getting an annual stipend from Trane & Co., according to Roland's letter to her, not that she wants for anything now. It reads like Roland wanted his departure to end the problems he left behind."

"It does read like that, Lee, but Roland was a dreamer, not a realist, and for sure in matters like this, we're not Roland. How long will it take for the police to determine whether he is dead or alive?"

"Uncle Harry isn't sure—months, years, never. But he believes the department will either bring Roland back or issue a death certificate within six months."

"Meanwhile, the news media are not aware that Roland and Mildred were on the verge of a marital split and that Roland has disappeared. That will change tomorrow morning when the report of his replacement in the play makes headlines. Their marital spats, as they were called, have appeared in gossip columns of late, and those stories and Roland's exit will open wide the door to a dirty laundry scandal, something Mildred Trane has dreaded and avoided for years."

"Well, it can't be helped."

Except for their thoughts, the walk back to Singer Couture after lunch was pleasant enough, with birds chirping in the sidewalk trees and the sun shining brightly. They were about to enter Singer Couture when Singer met them at the door, ushered them to a corner and began whispering.

"Poor Mildred! The police found a gun on the floor of Roland's empty closet. It must have fallen out of one of his coats. The gun, the bullets, they're the ones used to kill Suzie Sweet. Mildred is beside herself! She was married to a murderer! I told her she'll get sympathy galore, that it won't affect her career, but that didn't seem to be her concern. She wants out of tonight's performance. She can't allow this to affect her career, she can't. She must be brave and strong. The audience expects to see her, not an understudy. The news is devastating, true, but it may take her days, weeks, months to get over the news. My clothes on someone else for days, weeks, months? It must not be! It's not good for either one of us! Lee, Tenisha, go to her, speak to her. Our reputations are on the line. Such behavior would be unthinkable! You are relieved of your duties for the day."

"Mrs. Henderson is expecting—"

"I don't care what Mrs. Henderson is expecting! Margo will model the clothes she wants to see. Go quickly! In four hours at the latest, Mildred must be at the theater for the evening performance. We need your help!" And he walked them to the elevator, his hands holding theirs tightly until the elevator door opened. "Thank you! Thank you!" The door closed on Bernie Singer walking back to his office, mopping his brow.

"How does it feel to be needed?" asked Lily as they exited the building. Tenisha rolled her eyes upward in response, as Lily hailed a taxi.

Chapter Twenty-One

Lily and Tenisha cherished the rare days off that they could share together, but the headline in the morning paper propped up against the coffee pot was not conducive to enjoying their waffles and fruit:

NATIONWIDE MANHUNT ON
FOR HUSBAND OF MILDRED TRANE.

SECRET GIRLFRIEND MURDERED.
GUN FOUND ON FLOOR OF EMPTY CLOTHING CLOSET

"Sounds like the newspaper has already convicted him." Lily sighed as she refilled her friend's coffee cup.

"And, presumably, so have the police. The girlfriend certainly wasn't a secret to Mildred, not when divorce was on the horizon because of her."

"That story is yet to come, Ten. Tomorrow, I would guess. Poor Roland. He's given no identity—no name, no career—though his character is hinted at, and it's hardly favorable."

"The newspaper as purveyor of partial truths and pompous judgments. You and I know more, Lee, but not enough to stand in judgment on his character or his deeds."

"I'm glad Branten was with Mildred when we arrived last night. She appreciated his prompt response to her call. But he's another loose thread, or at least, his automobile is. What was it doing attempting to run down Jimmy Carlton, and why did he take so long to report its theft? The thief still hasn't been identified, you know. Uncle Harry says that's not unusual with stolen cars, but the choice of Jimmy Carlton as a victim could not have been an accident. It's too coincidental that both parties have a significant acquaintance with the Tranes."

"Significant, yes. Branten seems to have decided which Trane he will represent in court, if not in divorce proceedings, then in murder proceedings, but then, what choice did he have? Roland is gone, presumably for keeps. Not a shirt or tie was left behind."

The French telephone that Lily took such delight in rang, and she reached behind her for it. "Hello, Uncle Harry. Had your breakfast yet? Well, you should. Coffee is not enough to sustain you, and you should insist that Inspector Kirk honor your day off. What do you mean? Maybe he bought new clothes. What do you mean with what? He must have a bundle in the bank. He must have withdrawn the money. How else could he live incognito? That's absurd. He has to be alive. Not that big a coward! True. I don't know, but—yes, Uncle Harry, thanks for telling me. It was a gracious, favorite uncle thing to do. All right, all right. Goodbye." Lily turned to her friend. "Well, Ten, it was more than a favorite uncle thing. Unc wants information, and he wants us to get it. He and the good inspector think that Mildred may know where Roland is and is trying to protect him."

"If so, she certainly put on a good act at his disappearance. Of course, we know she's a great actress."

"And Uncle Harry says that the box office has been so besieged with requests for tickets that Edgar Davis intends to add additional performances, if Mildred promises to be in all of them. Her public would expect it."

"As a tag-along, that could up Roland's theatrical stock as well, and who knows? It might give reviewers and audiences second thoughts about the quality of Roland's revisions. Mildred might have colluded in his disappearance to get him increased favor for his work. There's nothing like a mystery to get creative juices of appreciation flowing. How do you propose we get information from Mildred? We offered to help her, not the police. Whose side are we on?"

"Bernie's. Her telephone will be tapped, and she will be followed, so we'll have to tune in to a higher power that has the answers. Not too high. I've already asked, and God doesn't want to get involved, so I beg his forgiveness, because we're going to less auspicious and questionable powers. If we go to enough of these, we may get some answers that are in the vicinity of the truth. It will be our judgment call."

"You can't be serious, Lee!"

Lily lay the telephone book in her friend's lap. "Psychics, your choice. Pen and paper are in the desk drawer. I'll pick up where you leave off after I've made more coffee. Some listings must be more convincing than others."

"Convincing? Ads are meant to be convincing. We want the truth! Well, Uncle Harry may have to do with convincing fiction. If Mildred can act, so can these supernatural specialists. Okay, okay, I don't have a better idea." And Tenisha turned the pages as the coffee pot sizzled.

*　　*　　*

"Won't Mildred wonder why only one of Roland's socks is in the laundry basket?" asked Tenisha.

"Wondering is the least of her problems. Besides, I don't think anyone in the household is in laundering mode, not for another day or so. Meanwhile, the sock may help us determine where he's run off to. Lucky I was able to snatch one before we left yesterday. We've got one Madame, one first name and one Mrs. Psychic. A good variety of types, and maybe techniques, Greenwich Village psychic number one, Madame Helene." Lily rang the bell.

A young woman with frizzled hair answered the door. She wiped her hands on her apron.

"Madame Helene is waiting. Thank you for being on time. Just a moment." She left them for a few minutes and then returned to walk them through the kitchen to a room at the rear of the brownstone. She knocked, paused, and opened the door.

Madame Helene came out from behind her desk, reached for their hands and held them for several seconds. "Welcome to my home. You are not related to the man you seek, I see. You have no personal interest in him at all. Why, then, are you here?"

"How do you know that?" challenged Tenisha.

"Your hands revealed as much to me. Well?" She returned to the chair behind her desk.

"We're helping a friend, an acquaintance, one of our boss's clients," said Lily.

"He trusts two young ladies," Madame Helene stated flatly.

"We've helped him before, when he wasn't asking for it. We did it for a friend, but it helped him too."

"Before, it was a murdered employee, and now it is a client's missing husband, is that not so?"

"You've been reading the newspapers," said Tenisha.

"I sensed the connection. I always meditate for half an hour before a client's arrival. I am glad you arrived on time. The sensation is more powerful that way. Have you brought anything of Mr. Trane's for my examination?" Lily handed her the sock.

"Unwashed. Excellent!" She closed her eyes and kneaded the sock with both hands. The room was dimly lit by a lamp on a table on one side of the room and a partially shuttered window on the other.

"He is near, but not nearby. He took a train to another big city. His looks are not the same. He is a very childish man and can easily be found, because he has not changed his ways."

"What city is Mr. Trane in, and what is he doing there?" asked Lily.

"Trane is a strong name for such a weak man. I do not see the city. I see him at a bank, in a luxury hotel suite, at a burlesque show. Are you sure his wife wants him back?"

"Can you see into her thoughts too?" asked Tenisha.

"No, the normal portion of my mind questions this."

"Will he eventually return home on his own?" asked Lily.

"He has no roots where he now resides." Madame Helene opened her eyes. "But do you think a man wanted for murder would feel secure if he does return? My conclusion is a practical not a psychic one. The man has a serious problem."

"Did Roland Trane murder Suzie Sweet?" asked Lily.

Madame Helene closed her eyes for what seemed forever, though not more than a minute elapsed before she responded. "No, he did not." She rose from her seat. "I'm glad that you came. I like to be of help, and I will eagerly follow the newspaper accounts to see how you have solved your case."

"Have you no confidence in the police?" asked Tenisha.

"For many things, yes. For this case, no. Goodbye, ladies. You may pay the young woman who admitted you."

"You trust your housemaid?"

"She is my daughter, Miss Chasen. She wears many hats. She judged you properly."

The psychic Georgette was also in Greenwich Village, but there was half an hour before their appointment. The two models strolled the area, looking through the windows of stores, bars and restaurants. At three o'clock they climbed the stairs to a second-floor apartment above a bicycle shop. The woman who admitted them was one they had seen through a bar window fifteen minutes earlier. She was the psychic Georgette. She asked them more questions than they asked her, and it became obvious to them that she was looking for clues that would allow her to give them what they wanted. Their responses were minimal, and judging by her conclusions, so were her psychic abilities.

They arrived unannounced at a commercial building in midtown Manhattan that was the home of medical and dental offices as well as insurance and accounting firms. The psychic Mrs. Weller would have had no opportunity to research her clients. Mrs. Weller opened the door herself, stared at them for a moment, and then asked what they wanted.

"You are listed in the telephone book as a serious psychic for serious people, and we need help," said Lily.

Mrs. Weller glanced from Lily to Tenisha and replied, "I do private work only, for individuals who need help with their lives. No divorces, scandalous situations or police work."

Is there anything left? thought the two women, but Lily responded, "We're searching for a missing person."

Mrs. Weller paused before replying, "My fees are rather steep, but if that is no deterrent, come in." She did not open the door wider, but waited.

Lily blotted out thoughts of an overdrawn account. "It is no deterrent."

Mrs. Weller's office was large, light and airy. The art deco furniture was offset here and there with Georgian chairs and porcelain bric a brac on shelves. The modern take on a traditional style might satisfy a wider range of clients. Perhaps Mrs. Weller found it pleasing herself. She pulled two straight-back Georgian chairs in front of her desk.

"Have you an item belonging to the missing person?" The sock was produced.

"You want to know this person's whereabouts. I will tell you what I see." She reclined in her chair and closed her eyes. After five minutes, Lily and Tenisha began to fidget, grateful that Mrs. Weller, eyes closed, could not see them. Mrs. Weller opened her eyes. "I regret to tell you that the party you seek is dead."

"But how? Where is he?" demanded Lily.

"I don't know where he is, but I see him lying on a bed in a hotel room. A bottle of pills is on the side table alongside a glass of water. I don't know how empty the bottle is or what is in it; I cannot read the label. The glass is partly full. I see its water line. It was filled to the brim. The clock reads 8 A.M. The 'Do Not Disturb' sign is on the inside door handle, so the maid will come in and find him."

"How do you know he's dead?" asked Tenisha.

"I see no breath, no respiratory movement."

"How long has he been lying there?" asked Lily.

"I cannot say, but he is in his pajamas, so possibly since the night before."

"Does the closet in the room contain clothing?" questioned Tenisha.

Mrs. Weller was quiet for a moment. "No, I see no clothing. I see a shirt, suit, and tie neatly placed on a chair. His shoes and socks are under them."

"Are the socks like the one you're holding?" asked Tenisha.

"Similar in design, but brown, not blue, a match for his suit."

"How would you characterize the hotel room?" asked Lily.

"Minimalist. Standard. Any other questions?"

Lily looked at Tenisha. "No. Your fee?" One weeks' salary was steep, but between them, the women managed to pay the bill with a little, very little, left over.

"We have enough for two cups of coffee and a small piece of cake to share. Then you'll have to call Ted for a ride home. I wish Donald had a car, because his history class will be over in half an hour, and Ted has two more hours to work."

"He'll leave earlier if I call. His father did supply fabric to Bernie for *The Ladder*, so he does have a stake in the play, and therefore in the one who revised as well as acted in it. At least, I hope he sees it that way. This coffee shop isn't crowded." They entered.

Seated in a corner booth, Lily began. "Well, what do you think? We can forget about Georgette. Fraud was written all over her face, and I'm not sure how much we can trust Mrs. Weller. I'm suspicious of a psychic who won't admit clients. We refused to be scared off by an outrageous fee, though if I had known what it was, I might have been!"

"Maybe she wondered if two young women could afford it. Maybe she thought that two women searching for a man would involve her in a scandalous situation. What concerns me more is that Madame Helene and Mrs. Weller didn't agree. Are we to believe that Roland Trane is dead or alive, that he's continuing his usual ways, or that he's moved on to a realm where the ways are quite different?"

"Well, we took a chance, Ten. We had no guarantee that psychics would be reliable. Madame Helene had our names, and a chance to check us out. Mrs. Weller did not. I don't know if that made a difference in what they told us. As for the big city they both agreed on, that doesn't tell us much. If a man wants to hide or do something nefarious, he's not likely to choose a small city, where everybody knows everybody else's business."

"Where's the nearest big city, Lee, or did they mean major?"

"Where? New Jersey, Connecticut, Pennsylvania? And what do we do, contact all the hotels in dozens of cities and ask if a man was found dead there recently or if they had a guest who might be Roland Trane, who probably changed his name and appearance before signing in?"

"He put the money he took out of the bank somewhere, and he took his clothes, hardly the actions of a man about to commit suicide. One up for Madame Helene. Call Ted, will you Lee?"

Ted arrived ten minutes later. He needed no permission from his father. He stated he was his own man, though happily his father had already left the office for the day. Lily entered her apartment to the ringing of the telephone. It was Bernard Singer.

"Mildred has been bombarded with thank-you calls from five charities. Roland donated some of his clothes to each of them. They will send her lists of the items and full notes of gratitude. She doesn't keep track of his clothes, so she won't know if he donated everything. He must have kept something."

If he planned to stay alive, yes, thought Lily.

"How is your search for Roland coming along?"

"Nothing definitive."

"Well, make it definitive. I don't want Mildred upset, at least not more upset than she is. She's not comfortable working with Roland's understudy. It's taken sheer determination for her to keep from thinking of Roland. This can have an effect on my clothes. Each has an identity of its own, and the wearer has to mesh with it, not with her problems."

"I thought clothes had to mesh with the wearer."

"That, too."

"But I still have to ask my clothes if I'm appropriate for them?"

"No, you don't wear Singers."

"I can't afford Singers, but if you'll give me some—"

"Forget what I said. I'll need you for a full day tomorrow. You may not get out until five o'clock. Get enough sleep."

"But tomorrow is my early day, and I have a four o'clock photo shoot at Lilly Daché."

"Lilly Daché! Lilly Daché! Lilly Daché! What is it with that woman? Your first obligation is to Singer Couture."

"I'll tell her that when I see her at four o'clock. Bye, bye Bernie."

Chapter Twenty-Two

"Mrs. Trane! How wonderful to see you here, and looking so well, in spite of . . . in spite of . . ." Lily trailed off.

"One can't mourn forever, Miss Chasen. I've shed tears enough for Roland, and I certainly can't keep the pact we made now. No replacement for him will be forthcoming from him, and the marital prospects I've selected for consideration are not as agreeable as I first thought. I have my career, and that's something, at least until some younger light showers sparks upon the stage and eclipses this old warhorse."

"You're still young!"

"Still, 'aye, there's the rub.' I could adapt, do older parts, even character roles; I don't mind adapting – too much, but when your star's eclipsed, it's eclipsed. I could try directing, but I'm not interested in directing. My voice would work well in sound films, which are the buzz of Hollywood and just around the corner, so they say. I think the romantic and heroic parts I've been blessed with will soon begin to elude me, and if such a part at our estate is in my future I see no sign of it. I'll enjoy what I have while I have it, and that obviously can no longer include Roland. Even arguing with him was an invigorating drama, but it is to be no more. You may never have to concern yourself with such a plight, or if you do, it's twenty years away. Do you know what I'm talking about?"

"Yes, I do, Mrs. Trane, but life is an exciting adventure that can have brilliantly unexpected results. You have to face it with happy expectations. You're more likely to detect happy possibilities that way. If you expect the worst, you may create self-fulfilling prophecies."

"I cannot change what I am or the way I look at life."

"You can change your environment and allow it to create new possibilities for you. You speak fluent French. Have you thought of starring on the Paris stage?"

"If I'm away for any length of time, I'll be forgotten. Roland forgot me while I was in London two years ago. Enter Suzie Sweet. It wasn't easy renewing the quality of plays I was offered before I left, either. But while my name is in the headlines and the gossip mills churn out slanderous comments too expensive to contest, my career is fine. Sad, isn't it?"

"Is there any way I can help?"

"Yes, you can allow me to come to terms with my dilemma. You can stop concerning yourself with my potential murderer. That issue has been resolved. You're searching for the murderer of Miss Sweet, and you can stop that too. It has no bearing on my life now, and the police are paid to do such jobs. Roland is gone, and perhaps it's for the best, so none of this matters anymore."

"And the attempted murder of your friend Jimmy Carlton?"

"Roland is gone, and Jimmy is alive. That's what matters."

"You think your husband tried to kill him?"

"William Branten said that Roland borrowed his car that day. He was vague about the hour, purposely vague, I think. The gun, of course, you know about. Roland's bullets matched those in Miss Sweet's body. Murderers don't make the best husbands. Anyway, I've come to thank you and Tenisha for working on my behalf, and to thank Bernie for forcing you both to do it. I know he's been concerned about my continued patronage, but he needn't be. He's a superb designer. Is he in his office?"

"Yes. His secretary left for a dental appointment, which I shouldn't be delaying myself, but my dentist is on vacation. Just knock, and go right in. He's always pleased to see you."

"If you need a dentist, there's one a healthy walk from here, one my Roland used." She opened her handbag for pencil and pad and wrote a name and address. "He's wonderful with emergency cases, very accommodating." And she turned away. Lily stared at the paper as Tenisha approached.

"Mildred Trane just expressed her gratitude to us. She seems to be holding up in these inflammatory days." Lily handed the paper to her friend. "Roland's dentist?"

"222 Sixth Avenue, #23. That's Mrs. Weller's building. It's the office next door!"

"With Roland gone, Mrs. Trane thinks there's no need for further investigation. I disagree. I could tell Uncle Harry and let the police follow up, but Mrs. Weller doesn't want notoriety, and since we don't know if she deserves our consideration, until we do know, I think she deserves the benefit of the doubt. Every newspaper in the city is at Inspector Kirk's heels about this case."

"We'll splurge on a taxi and eat our sandwiches en route to Dr. Snyder. Mrs. Weller requires another visit."

* * *

Dr. Snyder's secretary apologized for the delay, but lunchtime emergencies were getting more common. Lily and Tenisha had been waiting fifteen minutes, taking turns standing in the hallway outside the dentist's office. The floor had seen much traffic during that time, but no one had entered or left the Weller premises.

"Your neighbor seems to live on love. She doesn't get much traffic."

"Not during the day," said the secretary. "Her clients come when we've all left. She gets a very exclusive crowd, and they prefer not to be seen. Why tarnish their reputations when they can see her after dark? Oh, some come during the day, all muffled up, or in summer with dark glasses and heads down. It's kind of funny, but I hear she's good. Rich people don't keep patronizing losers. Some of our new patients have knocked on her door by mistake and been roughly shooed away. 'We're closed, we don't know you, who recommended you?' Comments like that."

"Who's the 'we?'"

"It's the royal 'we.' There's only Mrs. Weller. But she can be very nice. Occasionally we run short of coffee in the office, and if we slip a note under her door, she leaves a package in front of ours. She never comes in. She's only personal with her clients."

"How do you know how she behaves with her clients?"

"Some of our patients go to her, Miss Chasen. They say they only go for fun."

"With Roland Trane out of town, she'll have one client less," guessed Lily.

"Yes, and so will we! Such an unpleasant situation. I hope he's innocent. He's such a sweet, soft-spoken man. It's hard to believe he killed anyone or fooled around with a chorus girl. His wife is such a respectable person. It must be hard on her. His cosmetics are good, too. Have you tried them?"

"I use Helena Rubenstein," said Lily.

"I use Madam C.J. Walker," said Tenisha. "I have to support the family."

"Are you related to the Walkers?"

"My Aunt A'Lelia runs the company."

"Oooh! You're Mrs. Weller's kind of client."

Dr. Snyder beckoned Lily to enter, and at her exit fifteen minutes later, she borrowed pen and paper from the secretary and, with a firm hand, wrote the following message:

Mrs. Weller:

To avoid implication in a murder and the attendant scandal, it would be wise to see us immediately. We will not divulge the source of any information you give us, but if you refuse to see us, we will call the police. Answering to us will be safer.

We are waiting outside your door.

Two Models

Lily slipped the note under the psychic's door. She and Tenisha had to be back at work in half an hour, not too likely, but it would be foolish to leave now. Not more than two minutes elapsed before the door opened wide. Mrs. Weller stood boldly before them.

* * *

"So, Mrs. Weller was the informant, Lee."

"It's the only way Roland could have learned of Mildred's affair with Jimmy Carlton. He was so busy with other women, his wife would be his last concern. Of course he told Vivian. I'm glad it didn't affect her admiration for Mildred Trane, but after all, it was before she married Roland. Too bad he wasn't aware of that. Mrs. Weller should have told him, even if he didn't ask."

"Roland's foolish to think that if you disappear from your problems they'll disappear from you. Of course, if he murdered Suzie Sweet, he would have added incentive for disappearing, but did he seem like a murderer to you, Lee?"

"No, Ten, but appearances can be deceptive. Still, even a dreamer with unrealistic notions of love and marriage wouldn't be stupid enough to clear his closet and leave his gun with incriminating bullets on the floor. He didn't even clean off his fingerprints."

"Or somebody purposely didn't clean them off. Question: Did Roland Trane kill himself, as Mrs. Weller still insists, or is he roaming around somewhere in another place with another chorus girl, as Madame Helene says?"

"I think Mrs. Weller thinks of herself as a doctor, Ten. Despite our threats, I don't think she trusted us with the truth. I think that confidential information remains confidential with her. We tell the police that Roland is dead, as per her 'line,' and her client remains safe from arrest."

"Let's follow up on Madame Helene's vision. Let's start with a list of burlesque shows in major cities within easy driving distance of New York City and check for new boyfriends of girls in the chorus line."

"Good idea, Ten. The fact that Roland's only had two weeks to find a consoling head to lean on narrows the possibilities. Okay. Write this down: Englewood, Stamford, New Haven, Philadelphia, Providence and Newport. That's New Jersey, Connecticut, Pennsylvania, and Rhode Island. Let's knock out Englewood and Newport. Upscale places are not likely to have burlesque shows. Too bad we can't head to the New York Public Library to check out the telephone books, but we're half an hour late back to work already."

"The blame-game is moving too fast, Lee. Let's go to the library now. We can plead Mildred Trane. Best client, name in lights, all of that. And you'd avoid another excuse, valid or not, for leaving for Lilly Daché or anyone else before five o'clock."

"You're either psychic or you've looked at my appointment calendar. Let's go."

The institution protected by marble lions welcomed them into its vast space and illuminating archives. They headed for the telephone books. With the numbers of a dozen burlesque enterprises, they headed for Singer Couture and an irate boss. They lunched at work the next day, alternating between sandwich bites and telephone calls, praying the boss wouldn't barge in on them and dock them for the cost of long-distance calls. Both women worked from the same script:

"I'm looking for one of your chorines who has a new boyfriend. As I was cleaning, I found an expensive bracelet he bought her. He's left for a business conference, and I don't want to be responsible for it. If there's someone with a new boyfriend, I'd appreciate her name and telephone number."

That was their line. It yielded six responses—three names and numbers and three requests for the name of the boyfriend, his telephone number, and the name of his "maid." They repaired to the lounge to compare notes.

"One woman was guarded in her response, and two refused outright to talk. A suspicious bunch, and we're such pleasant, harmless inquisitors. What have you got, Ten?"

"One chorine said she wished her boyfriend could afford an expensive bracelet, another said she got a necklace, took it home when she left, and doesn't think it cost more than one dollar. The remaining chorine couldn't be reached. She's away, on loan to the National Burlesque Company that's doing a one-week stint in New York City. Her home company allowed her to go because she insisted. She thinks strutting her stuff in New York will advance her career. She's their best girl, and they didn't want to lose her permanently."

"If she's got a chance with a national company, it's a wonder she doesn't leave anyway."

"They're national in name only, Lee. Hope springs eternal. I've been trying, without success, to reach someone in the boardinghouse the company is staying at. They must be rehearsing like crazy. They open tomorrow night."

Bernard Singer appeared in the lounge doorway. "Your uncle is here to see you, Lee."

Detective Harry Chasen entered the lounge and removed his hat. "Hello, girls. Be advised that Inspector Kirk is on the rampage. He's going to find Roland Trane if he has to turn the country upside down, but he's trying to contain himself in front of Mildred Trane, whom he's had in for questioning. You know how much he admires her as an actress, and he doesn't want to be the cause of a poor performance in *The Ladder*. It's obvious she's under a strain, even though Roland was a worthless husband. I just came by to tell you we can't have dinner tonight, Lily. I wish we could, but a murder case just dropped in our laps. You'd think that women from the City of Brotherly Love would have the consideration to be murdered at home, not on a visit to New York."

Tenisha sat bolt upright. "Who is she?"

"We don't know. She had no identification on her. She was wearing a dress and hose that had seen better days, and a hat, a stunning Lilly Daché hat, so said the label inside. She couldn't have afforded it. If we can find out her name and who bought the hat for her, it would help us a lot."

"Was she with the National Burlesque Company?"

"You must be psychic, Tenisha!"

Lily winced. "They must know her name."

"They know her stage name, Lavinia Lake. She was on loan to them, but her home company doesn't know more about her."

"I'm making an encore visit to Lilly Daché after work. One of the hats I was to model last time wasn't finished. I'll ask Miss Daché."

"Thanks, honey. I'll call to reset our dinner date. When I retire in a few years, we'll dine together often, if you'll have the time, that is. You'll probably be a famous opera star by then, and I'll have to wait until *you* retire!" He kissed his niece and left.

"Roland has an eye for star-quality chorines, and he might just be angry enough to buy Lavinia Lake a hat from a milliner his wife dislikes!" Lily sighed.

Bernard Singer loomed large in the doorway. "Lee, Tenisha, Mildred Trane begs to see you immediately at her home. She's having some sort of meeting and says your presence is urgently required. Enough is enough, and I almost told her so! This is a fashion house, not a hiring hall! What can't wait, what is so important that it disrupts our workday? I need you both now! Mrs. Jameson is coming in for a private viewing and wants you, Lee. Mrs. Johnson wants to swagger and says only you, Tenisha, can do it in the dresses I sketched for her. These impositions from make-believe land are an outrage! When will some people realize we're trying to run a business, and that the fashion world does not ignore the demands of real life, and those living in the fantasy world of the stage have no right to ignore it either."

"'So, what did you tell Mildred Trane, Bernie?"

"I told her you and Tenisha would be right over. Tell her to get a grip, will you? I don't know how much more of this I can take. Every day, it's Roland this, Roland that, and danger, fears, threats, the police…." Singer continued muttering down the hall.

"We always knew the fashion world was insane, but ours is getting insaner by the minute. Get our jackets, will you, Ten? I want to make a call." She dialed the telephone in the lounge. "Hi, Uncle Harry. Can you drop off that Daché hat at Miss Daché's at four o'clock? I know it's evidence, but you want answers, don't you? Ask her yourself, if you'd like. Of course, she can't be expected to know who buys every one of her hats throughout the country. She's not psychic, but she may be able to shed some light that will help you. Yes, I know her. That doesn't mean she won't cooperate with you. You're the police, for goodness sake. Embarrassed? She makes hats, not undergarments. Will you drop off the hat or not? I'm sure you'll find a way. Thank you." Lily hung up. "Men!"

*   *   *

Mildred Trane controlled her agitation as best she could, but she was breathing hard when she opened the door for Lily and Tenisha. Faithful Roderick, her butler, was nowhere in sight. She led the models into the Victorian library. Producer Edgar Davis and attorney William Branten were seated on the sofa and turned as the women entered. A porcelain urn sat on the table before them. The women seated themselves on damask chairs around the table with its lone object.

"Roland has returned. He ordered this sent to me with an accompanying letter." Mildred Trane produced it and handed it to the two women, who put their heads together to read it:

My Dearest,

I wish I could have found another way to resolve our differences, but this was more final than any other. What good qualities you continued to see in me for ten years that kept you by my side elude me. I am grateful for those years, but it is unfair to continue to enjoy your faithfulness while I continue my infidelities. And they would continue; I cannot change. That is what I would have told all my future marital prospects, but there is no need for that now. Forgive me for my many falls from grace, as I forgive an occasional and justifiable slip from you. I leave you financially secure.

I hope you will continue your friendship with my dear sister. I know in my bones, or shall I say my ashes, that she will do a better job of running Trane & Co. than I ever could. Some people just have the knack for success, in the workplace, at home and in life.

Console my mother, who adores you. I'll never leave you now. From here on, consider me a past decoration in your life. I'm sure our life together has strengthened you for any rough spots that lay ahead. May they be few! Mourn neither the past nor the present.

The future lies ahead!

Love.
Roland

"How did you get this letter?" asked Lily.

"It was conveyed by the landlady of the small hotel to the mortician, and eventually on to me."

"How can you be sure this is Roland?"

William Branten spoke. "We can't be sure, Miss Chasen, but the landlady clearly identified Roland, although he was using a different name, as the dying man who had given her the instructions. This letter was in a sealed envelope inside a larger envelope, so neither she nor the mortician knew immediately what it contained."

"Weren't the police called?" asked Tenisha.

"Of course, and they determined his identity by the bank book in his pocket. It was from a local bank. They opened the sealed letter and forwarded it to his next of kin, whose name and address were printed in pencil on the larger envelope. She effected the cremation and forwarded the remains to Mrs. Trane with the letter you've just read. Roland recorded his next of kin as one Lavinia Lake. Since he expired in the ambulance and there were witnesses to his demise and request about his remains and the letter, the police saw no need to question his departure from this world."

"Or to notify the New York City police department about it. When did his death take place?"

"The coroner has determined it was two days ago, Miss Jones. You see the predicament this creates for Mrs. Trane."

"And *The Ladder*," added the producer.

"The police assured me," said Mildred Trane, "that the discovery of Roland's gun, his disenchantment with Miss Sweet, his borrowing of Mr. Branten's automobile the very day Jimmy Carlton was attacked by the vehicle, and his hasty departure clearly pointed to his murder of Miss Sweet and the attempted murder of Mr. Carlton, who had been seen deep in conversation with Miss Sweet, learning who knows what displeasing facts Roland would have liked suppressed."

"Although the evidence is strong, it is completely circumstantial," said William Branten, "and I would have decimated police conclusions in a court of law. However, Roland saw fit not to make that necessary, bless his soul. Misguided though he was, he was a good man."

"Roland is dead," exclaimed an anguished Mildred Trane, "and can't be tried in a court of law, not on earth, anyway, but I can be! The onus of the murder now rests on me! I killed Roland because I was fed up with his affairs. I killed Suzie Sweet because she insulted me with her liaison with Roland, and I borrowed William's car after Roland returned it so I could kill the man who would reveal we'd had an affair, and I'd be unable to prove it was before I married Roland. Roland could have destroyed my reputation, my financial security, made William's defense of me look biased, and made me want to commit suicide. What would I have to live for? That's what the police will say. With Roland dead, I stand to inherit two-thirds of his estate, not the one-third I would have received in a divorce. Circumstantial evidence galore, but powerful. Can I trust a jury of my peers to acquit me, and even if they should, can I trust any producer to star me in any play—ever?"

"Without Mrs. Trane, *The Ladder* will die a second death. She brings the script to life. She imprints the message on the hearts of the audience. We cannot allow lies to ruin her life or the play's," insisted Edgar Davis.

"Our only hope is to find Lavinia Lake," said Mildred, "but those at her building address didn't know her. There's no trace of parents or relatives."

"Lavinia Lake has been found in New York, Mrs. Trane. She was part of a visiting burlesque company."

"Where can I reach her, Miss Chasen?"

"She's in the city morgue, Mr. Branten. She's been murdered."

"Will they blame that on me, too?"

"Calm down, Mildred." William Branten turned toward Lily and Tenisha. "Who else is aware of her connection to Roland?"

"No one outside this room, not even the police. My uncle, Detective Harry Chasen, mentioned her name when he begged off dinner with me. Neither the company she was traveling with nor her home company knows her real name. The police department will investigate, but her death is likely to be one of the many recorded, but unsolved."

"Whoever murdered her may be responsible for the murder and attempted murders that concern us, but we face the same dead end as the police."

"Perhaps not, Mr. Branten. Ten and I may be able to help because of some information my uncle inadvertently revealed. We won't say more just now, but if you don't inform the police about the urn, you may continue your life as before, Mrs. Trane, and you your play, Mr. Davis."

"As the family attorney, I think you should tell me what you've found out."

"Soon enough, Mr. Branten," said Lily, "but I'm sure you can appreciate our wish to present facts, not circumstantial evidence. There's been enough of that already."

The two models stood, and Mrs. Trane quickly stood too, and grabbed their hands in fervent appreciation.

"I must be the first to know," insisted William Branten.

Lily and Tenisha looked at each other in unspoken agreement. This insistence was from a "family" attorney, who only recently couldn't decide which Trane to favor. Lily dialed for two taxis, one for Tenisha, who was headed home, and one for herself. She might arrive at Miss Daché's just when Uncle Harry did. She wondered how much about his situation Roland Trane had told Lavina Lake. Probably not too much; his letter to his wife had not included Miss Lake's name. He probably hadn't revealed the extent of his wealth, either. The name David West, Roland's nom de plume, wouldn't conjure up a fortune in a woman's mind. How had he planned to fund his retirement from Trane & Co.? Branten had not divulged any written instructions he had received now or in the past, assuming Roland had eerily foreseen the present, presumably with Mrs. Weller's help. Lily leaned forward in the taxi. "Driver, here please." She paid him, exited the taxi and looked up at the tall building Daché had built right in the heart of this exciting city. Not many years past, she had been a French immigrant, with no knowledge of English and very little money. Now she lived in a penthouse apartment above this gorgeous space and was hailed throughout the country, throughout the world, for her hats. Uncle Harry was in the lobby holding a box.

"Be careful with this, Lily. I'd like it back as soon as possible, preferably before Inspector Kirk notices it's missing. Not that he'd fault me for taking it, but Miss Daché might fault me for exposing her to the not-always-gracious inspector, and you for sure would! Call me as soon as you can with the results."

Miss Daché was in her workroom creating a hat meant to be worn to one side of the head. Flowing from the back was a long, lovely streamer. She looked up at the model she was expecting.

"A rayon ribbon might be best," she announced. "A removable one might be even better and make the hat more versatile, unlike Elsa Schiaparelli's streamer skirt on the Bernard Singer dress she modified at his showing last week. Three clients told me stories about her performance. I appreciated hearing them. Millinery ideas come from everywhere!" She looked at Lily's box,

"A gift for me? I hope it isn't a hat!"

"It is!" Lily explained its purpose.

Miss Daché put down her newest creation, lifted the hat in one hand and a pair of scissors in the other and snipped lose the label announcing her authorship. "There's a number on the back of each label indicating the store to which it was sold. You say the gentleman has been gone less than two weeks. It would take at least that long to receive checks for a new checking account. Most likely he paid cash. If he had it delivered, there should be a record of his name, as well as the recipient's. If he hand-delivered it himself, proof of his identity would have to come from a salesgirl with a good memory. Not impossible." She telephoned her sales office with one hand, turning her latest creation every which way for examination with her other hand, "Michele? Yes, what store did we sell this item to?" She read Michele the number. "And how many did we sell them and when?" She waited, drumming one hand impatiently on the table. "Thank you." She turned to Lily. "One hat of this particular style was delivered three weeks ago to Lord & Taylor in Philadelphia." She dialed again. "Millinery, please." More drumming. "Isn't anyone there? Well, please take this down. I would like the salesgirl who sold it to identify the person who bought it." She repeated the number. "Have her call me, please, when she returns. Lilly Daché. Yes, *the*

Lilly Daché. Thank you." She turned to Lily. "The sales staff is on strike. I once endured a similar attempt to keep customers away, not from my girls, but from the union that wanted my girls as members. This shop was picketed for months by outsiders. Regardless of the weather, there they were, trying to keep my clients and my girls away. But they didn't succeed. I housed my girls on the premises. We got to know one another quite well! What loyal darlings they are, and my clients came anyway. My husband was very patient and understanding. The union finally gave up. But union contract demands are not the same as union membership demands, so I doubt that the department store will be without staff or customers for very long. Their own employees are marching outside, and they are not getting paid. My dear Lily, your head is very valuable to me. I would like to continue to see it on your shoulders. Pierre should have the camera and scenery in place, but I will not budge until you have told me the whole story."

Lilly Daché listened intently as Lily Chasen spoke. When an assistant balancing four hats in various stages of completion entered the room, she motioned the girl away. When Lily's recitation of events had ended, the milliner sighed.

"Even though Mrs. Trane is not a client, I feel sorry for her. She will be lonely without her husband. If he is alive, but not with her, that is a bearable loneliness; there is always a chance of his return. But death is final. One is left with memories, which may be better than the real thing, but they do not feel better. When I first came to New York City, I was too busy to be lonely. I was in love with a city and did not need a man. As Mrs. Trane began her career, the joy of it, the thrill of new roles was probably enough. After a while, she may have thought, as I did, that it would be nice to have somebody to talk to, somebody who would take me to a gay place, perhaps to dance. So, one Saturday I went to the subway, looking for adventure. I had just quit my job at Macy's because they had ordered me to sell hats whether they suited the customer or not. They were only interested in a sale; the customer did not matter. But the customer mattered to me. Since I was six years old in France, the lady who would wear the hat I made mattered. So, in this exciting city of New York in the subway, I took the first train that came along.

I got on it and hung to a strap along with the crowds. I didn't notice where it was going at first, but I thought: I will ride to the end of the line and see where it is. Then I will get out and explore, and that will be an adventure. I met a man that way, a nice one, too! Mrs. Trane probably took the first train that came along. Perhaps she was moving too fast in her career to have any time to hear marriage proposals. Perhaps none was offered. She was fortunate that the man she married was wealthy and seemed kind. I would think that he could dance, too. When he started secret friendships with other women, she hung onto the train strap. In France, women would not take such detours too hard. They may take detours of their own, but I can understand her feelings. I would take it hard, too, and I would not be quiet about it either. But she rode the train to the end of the line, and now she sees where it is, and it is not in a pretty place. She must with reluctance get off the train. But will she have a chance to explore, to have a new adventure? That may be decided for her, but you have a chance to help her. You put your life in danger by doing so, but you have no choice. You want to be an opera singer, and fate led you to begin modeling and singing clothes onstage at Bernard Singer Couture. Fate led you to me, and I am very grateful. It seems that the reputation that will lead you to your dream is coming through a side door. You and your friend's solution to the Lizette Frere murder case last year got you plaudits as detectives, but also got you name recognition, not for music, true, but recognition, nonetheless. And now this! The Tranes are not strangers to Philadelphia. When I was in that city on business, I attended one of Mrs. Trane's performances and went backstage to congratulate her on her superb characterization of the female lead. Her husband was in her shadow that night, as would be expected, but it was she who knew the city's socialites. I assume he's had business dealings there, as have I, but he did not seem comfortable in the social scene. I am guessing that, like me, he goes to Philadelphia for reasons of work and then goes home. I don't know this for certain, of course, but Mildred Trane is certainly known and adored in that city. If the police knew that she had her husband's ashes in her possession, that they appeared, shall we say, out of nowhere, they might question whether she's told them all she knows about Mr. Trane's disappearance. They might surmise that she got someone to hire a chorus girl to entice her husband, poison him, forge a letter with his signature and mail his ashes to his wife, who would have the last laugh, as you say, keeping her husband and avoiding a divorce, which in court would lead to revealing his embarrassing escapades. She is provided with a significant inheritance, double, you tell me, what she would have received in a divorce. If people in contact with Mr. Trane in his bogus identity saw him as happy and not a suicide prospect, Mrs. Trane would not be in an enviable position."

"Forgery is a talent that's not easily acquired."

"You are right. It is my imagination that does the talking."

Miss Daché's eyes, intently gazing into Lily's, gleamed. "You will be victorious in this adventure. I feel it." She twirled Lavinia Lake's hat in one hand. "This chapeau and I will help you. Your life was meant to take this turn, as mine was meant to come to America to do this." She opened her hands wide, embracing the room.

Lily opened her purse and took out a carefully folded paper. "You said this in a magazine interview, and I saved it. I read it whenever I question why I follow a dream, and what I'm doing in New York." She handed the paper to Miss Daché, who read aloud:

"Now when I look back to those first months in New York, and all the years since, it seems to me my life has unrolled like a ribbon, with a certain pattern. Maybe the pattern was already woven when I was born, and all I had to do was unroll the spool. I do not know. But this I do know—that always there has been something pushing me on, so that I could not have stopped to take another road, even if I had wanted to."

Lily Ann Chasen hugged the greatest milliner in the world who, with a catch in her voice, said, "Come!" taking Lily by the hand and leading her to the photo shoot that awaited her.

*   *   *

Lily entered her apartment to the ringing of the telephone. "Hi, my darling niece. I thought you'd want to know that Lavinia Lake slipped and revealed one of her past identities. She wrote Lavinia Lake, aka Joyce Lambert on a bank loan application. Miss Lake, who had no money to speak of, was unable to get a loan, but Miss Lambert, who had a nice chunk of money in a bank in Illinois, could and did. She's wanted for forgery in several states. Any news from her hat?"

"It was bought in a department store in Philadelphia for cash, but the staff is on strike, so date of purchase is unknown as is the physical description of the buyer."

"Let's hope the strike ends soon. Inspector Kirk would like to talk to Mrs. Trane, not interrogate his favorite actress, mind you, but she is reluctant to oblige. Heavier than expected performance schedule, nervous exhaustion, distraught condition concerning Roland, and all that. Her physician doesn't want her disturbed for the duration."

"What duration?"

"Probably the duration of uncertainty about what happened to Roland Trane and who was responsible for it. The inspector doesn't want to accuse her of anything, can't really, even though she has friends in Philadelphia, and with friends, almost anything is possible. I had to explain about the missing hat, and he's willing to wait until Miss Daché can provide some answers, through you, believe it or not. I think he respects you more than he's letting on."

Lily thought of the ashes. "It's hard to stay on the good side of the inspector," she muttered.

*   *   *

"Good evening, Roderick. Is Mrs. Trane at home?"

"No, Inspector, but she should be here soon. May I get you something, sir? Tea, perhaps?"

"Yes, thank you." Inspector Kirk walked into the living room and sat down with relief. It had been a long day. Since the Trane troubles had begun, he had been to their home many times. He looked around the Victorian room with admiration. Those bygone days were quiet times, settled times, conservative times. One could come home and not worry about the state of the country or the world. His eyes settled on something he had not seen before, and he got up to examine it. The porcelain urn sported an ornate design that was not displeasing. He picked it up. It was heavier than he thought. He opened the lid and peered within it, then reached inside. The ashes filtered through his fingers. He turned to Roderick, who had stopped short in the doorway holding a pot of tea and a plate of cookies on a tray.

"What is this?"

Chapter Twenty-Three

A 'Lelia Walker reclined on the living room sofa, glad that she had the day to herself. She had hosted a party the previous night for Langston Hughes. It had been awesome, but debilitating.

Looking through the window at the city trees on the sidewalk outside her Harlem home, she determined the time had come to commence a summer communing with nature, strolling through the gardens and taking long, delightful walks at her Irvington estate. When she was called to the telephone, Harlem's grand hostess and cosmetics heiress decided she would not accept a return of hospitality this night.

"Tenisha, my darling niece! It's been weeks since you called your favorite aunt. Yes, I seem to be in a never-ending social season, but you mustn't mind the newspaper accounts. I always have time for you. Of course, I've been following the Trane scandal. Who hasn't? I took a dozen writers to the performance three days ago, and we had a wonderful time discussing it at a party here afterwards. A diversity of opinions about the production, but no one faulted Mildred Trane, one of your clients at Singer, I know, darling. I can't have anyone over tonight. I'm exhausted, and—what do you mean Lizette Frere all over again only worse? Oh, dear! Ashes, you say? Yes, but last year I wasn't harboring a—I know she's not a criminal, not officially, but even for a few days ... Why doesn't she use a cosmetician from her husband's company, late husband's? Of course, my cosmetics are used by performers all over the globe! The Cotton Club is pleased. I've had no complaints from France; Josephine Baker is satisfied. If my friends hear of this, they will—what do you mean increase? Now look here, Tenisha, I ..." A'Lelia Walker held one hand on the telephone and the other over her eyes as she listened to her niece-turned-lawyer, or so it seemed, rattle on. "All right, but as soon as the police have a warrant for her arrest, I'll be on the telephone immediately. Better the telephone than the jail. You're not even coming with her? Do your parents know what you're doing? Tenisha!"

"She hung up. That girl can drive me to distraction! Not often, it's true, but when she does... Well, she's the only Negro model at a major American couturier. I can't spoil it for her by refusing to help one of their major clients, who also happens to be the talk of the town. I should have Mildred Trane to one of my soirées," she mused. "She would make a grand entrance and—I'd better clear my dressing table and have appropriate cosmetics ready when she arrives. We'll have to make do with the selection I have. Does Tenisha think I run a factory in the house?"

*   *   *

Lily and Tenisha passed a patrolman they recognized on their way into the theater.

"Didn't you ladies see the play opening night?"

"It's worth seeing again," said Lily. They were there to make sure Mildred Trane's exit after the performance would go undetected by the police, although Inspector Kirk had secured the front and stage entrances with one patrolman apiece, not enough to alert the ever-present press that he wanted to talk to Mildred Trane, though he wanted to talk to Mildred Trane. Roderick, at Mrs. Trane's request, had shown the inspector Roland's letter, with Roland's unmistakable signature. He had no cause, as yet, to arrest her and intensify the scandalous talk about her, but he had considerable cause to speak to her. Her reluctance to speak to him he did not attribute to guilt of any kind as yet, but to a desire to wait for information about a hat, and to keep from further agitation before her performances. The inspector didn't want to be responsible for ruining a performance, and certainly not for ruining a distinguished career, but he had a responsibility to the department and to all New Yorkers to do what he was paid to do, to be a credit to the title he bore. Unless one of his men apprehended the actress exiting the theater, he would speak to her in the privacy of her home, outside of which he also had men stationed. He would not push her into unwanted conversation, though he felt the looks the chief of police had given him of late were a "push" of their own.

The director was onstage, approving a few new touches to the drapes. This was as it had been in the days of failure, when little changes here and there had been made in the belief that minor improvements would create miracles and catapult the play into the stratosphere of success. Occasional dialogue had been changed then, too, but that was deemed too risky when the star was under so much pressure from other quarters. Anyway, she had insisted on a script without further changes once the play re-opened, and her wishes had been granted. Lily and Tenisha were shown the pathway through which Mrs. Trane would enter and leave the theater. It was through an underground passage that emerged into daylight or moonlight from a small building down the block. From there the star would be whisked via the producer's car to the lavish Harlem residence of A'Lelia Walker. The models turned to see Vivian and her mother approaching them. The exuberance of the week before was gone. Wan smiles all around.

"We're here to support Mildred," said the matriarch. "I consider her my daughter as much as Roland is my son." They sat on lobby chairs that the crowd waiting outside would not occupy for another fifty minutes. "We've heard it all," said Elizabeth Trane, "and believe none of it. Roland is not dead, and Mildred is not culpable for anything, except for staying with Roland this long. It's what has kept him from behaving even worse, though his behavior has been bad enough. Marriage vows mean nothing anymore. In my day—but what's the use of looking back? My day is gone, and not likely to return. At least there is someone close to Roland we can rely on. William Branten has behaved more like a friend than an attorney."

"I'm glad to hear it," said Lily, "so I hope you won't mind sharing with us, Vivian, what you overheard Mr. Branten and Mr. Carlton talking about during intermission on opening night."

"Oh, it was just talk about their summer vacations. Mr. Carlton said his family will be spending a week in Newport, and Mr. Branten said that this year his family will not be spending more than a week there either. Too busy."

"Too busy or too broke?"

"Really, Lily Ann Chasen! I'm sure Trane & Co. compensates him generously, and he does have a personal practice too, you know. He's been very kind. He has advised me of my rights and privileges as heir presumptive of Trane & Co., and he agrees with Roland that I could do better than he in management, in advertising, in ways I could not imagine. He was very optimistic about my abilities, my intelligence, my quickness to learn. It was all very flattering. I would like to believe him."

"So would most women," responded Lily.

"I'm surprised you're not asking me what I overheard Willie Simpson and Robert Blair say during intermission."

"All right, I'm asking."

"They were in competition as to who could say more flattering words about Mildred's performance." Vivian stamped a foot. "I want Roland back! He has to be alive, and he's got to come back! I was just beginning to know him, to like him. I don't want to take charge of Trane & Co., not now. I want time to grow, to enjoy being young. I can be a businesswoman when I'm older, much older." Vivian turned to Tenisha. "Maybe then your Aunt A'Lelia would be willing to help me, though why she should be willing to help competition is beyond me."

"Oh, she helps competition!"

"Is she helping Mildred?"

Tenisha bit her tongue, then whispered, "Auntie is applying Mildred's makeup. The police have staked out this theater, and if they see her enter and approach to question her, she will have no choice but to respond. She doesn't want to speak either before or after a performance, to them or to the press until we know what has happened to Roland."

"No wonder she's not in the theater yet, but how will she arrive and depart without detection by the police?"

A bell rang in the lobby. "She's in!" exclaimed Tenisha.

"Secret passage!" exclaimed Vivian.

"Lucky you're not on the police force," said Lily. "You said that Branten was supportive. You know he said he was not sure whom he would represent in divorce proceedings, Roland or Mildred."

"Yes, he told me. He was hoping he could represent them both, if they agreed. I can understand his feelings. Mine are the same too. He even postponed attending to some urgent personal business so he could be here with us."

"What was so urgent?"

"He didn't say, except that he would have to be out of the country for at least a week. His personal business is his personal business."

"He gets paid well enough, I would imagine, for him to stay here for you."

"Oh, Lily, don't be so cynical. There are still some good men around, even if Mama has kept me so close I haven't had a chance to find them."

"Where?" Then Lily thought of Ted and Donald. "I stand corrected," she responded. "Possibly."

The performance went well. An air of passion permeated Mildred Trane's characterizations, and the audience knew why and appreciated it. The secret exit went well and just in time, for, finding Mildred Trane gone, Inspector Kirk investigated and found the secret route. For the next evening performance, another entrance and exit would have to be devised. Mildred Trane and A'Lelia Walker were enjoying a late evening discussion of face, form and fashion design, because when Tenisha called half an hour before midnight, her aunt cut her short to continue what she said was a brilliant argument in favor of French fashion. The next day at lunchtime, Lily called Elsa Schiaparelli, who had just returned the night before to Paris from her American visit.

"Any purchases of late from William Branten?" she asked.

"Yes. He allowed purchases by a young lady he was here with last summer, a French model, who returned to her parents in Paris after working in the United States for a year. She looked sixteen last year, and my staff says she didn't look any older this year. Why do some adults refuse to give children a chance to grow up? Branten gave a top figure he would be responsible for, but changed it to the number of dresses rather than an amount in francs when he was told that a French manufacturer had offered to spend a great deal more on the young lady. By not being here, he could not deny her a purchase by claiming that it did not look attractive on her. The manufacturer was by her side when she came in a few days earlier. The child cost both gentlemen a prodigious amount. They would have had a better chance at reasonable expenditures had they brought their wives rather than their mistresses, and they would have had a sense of permanency in the relationship for the francs spent. Why didn't Mr. Branten come?"

"He had to preserve his bread and butter income. There are changes afoot in the personal and business affairs of Trane & Co.'s president and CEO."

"So I would imagine. I await more juicy news to come. I assume you are also calling because Tenisha Jones is not ready to say 'oui' to my business proposal?"

"You assume correctly. I'm sorry to have interrupted your catching up on business with questions about people."

"No need to apologize. I'm glad to reply. People are my business. Who else would I be making clothes for?" A parrot repeated her words. "Quiet!" she shouted at him. "I must go. Goodbye." There was a click, and the designer was gone.

Lily was on her way to a photo shoot for Kayser Stockings. She wore them herself. The double heel made the leg look long and attractive. Whether in beige, grey or black, they were a "must" in any woman's wardrobe. She would be looking backward at the viewer with her leg extended, so she had been advised to wear something appropriate. She had decided on a nubby, white boucle summer suit. She had gotten a seat on the bus, so the jostling around her as the bus filled did not disturb her, but her thoughts did. One murder had been committed, and two had been attempted, with two additional attempts presumed, which had started the roller coaster investigation to determine who had been responsible for them. Suzie Sweet, fiancée of the married Roland Trane, had been murdered. An attempt had been made to kill Mrs. Trane in the theater, and in the street, her devoted friend, former lover and renowned drama critic Jimmy Carlton had been targeted by a car stolen from Trane attorney William Branten.

Before these events, Roland Trane believed that someone had pulled the library ladder out from under him, leaving him momentarily dangling, and Mildred Trane at that very time believed that someone had tried to kill her by applying pressure in the small of her back as she was about to descend the mansion stairs to go to Roland's aid at his shout for help. The initial fears of devilish activity were mere assumptions, but the murder and two near murders were not. Who would gain by having Suzie Sweet dead? Mildred, surely. Her death would stop divorce proceedings in their tracks. There would be no reason for them, at least until Roland found someone else for the extramarital activities for which he had a proclivity. Roland himself might benefit, if Ms. Sweet's crass behavior toward his lovely sister nullified her appeal to him, because her death would provide him with an easy exit from a verbal obligation. Shooting her seemed a bit overkill, however, to affect her departure from his world. Who would benefit from Mildred Trane's death? Surely Roland Trane, who could then marry Suzie Sweet, or anyone else who took his fancy, without relinquishing any of his fortune to do so. Who would benefit from killing Jimmy Carlton? Roland Trane could erase images of an affair between the writer and Mildred by erasing him from life. William Branten could prevent embarrassment if the writer, known for his devastating attacks on people's theater performances, had been informed by the never-diplomatic Ms. Sweet that she had been Branten's mistress shortly before becoming Roland's. How Mrs. Branten would react to this news was another consideration. The two initial threats, with nothing to corroborate them, might merely be the product of overworked imaginations, and the disappearance and reappearance of a green bracelet were not suspicious enough to make anyone think of murderous intentions behind them, and yet they did. Whatever motives were behind them did not warrant murder, but did any motives ever warrant it? Lily got off the bus for a short stroll to the Keyser building.

*   *   *

Lily was about to exit Keyser when she was beckoned to the telephone. "Miss Daché called earlier, but you had already started the modeling session."

"Lily, come now," said Daché. "I have the news, I have the hat, I have the clipping." Click. Lily Ann Chasen hurried to the street and hailed a taxi. She felt what followed would be worth the expense. Miss Daché was in an even more excited mode than usual.

"The hat was bought on May 28 by a Mr. David West, or so he signed the card he asked to be delivered to Miss Lavinia Lake. He then thought better of it and said he would give her the gift himself. He wanted to see the look on her face when she opened the package. The salesgirl remembered him well. She said she had never had a customer who lost half his mustache when he bent to sign a card, or whose beard fell off when it caught on a Daché spike from another hat on the counter. You see what detective work my hat has done?" Lilly Daché's eyes twinkled. "You said the day of cremation was May 27. I am pleased that even the dead cannot resist returning for a Daché. Look here." She placed an advertisement from the morning newspaper in Lily's hands:

THE NATIONAL BURLESQUE COMPANY
Presents A Rising Star
LAVINIA LAKE
in
TIMELY STITCHES
A Serious But Provocative Review
Not To Be Missed!!

"I called the National Burlesque Company. It was too late for them to stop the advertisement. No newspaper is yet aware of her death. Can Mr. West be aware of it?"

"Even our police department isn't."

"Mr. West/Trane would not have killed her. You do not kill someone you have just gifted with an expensive Daché hat. So the dead can return in safety to see a show, can they not? Then you be there to see it too. Will you take the hat, will you take the ad? I have a business to run!"

*   *   *

Lily rued the expense of the day as she exited the taxi in front of the Cort Theatre. A strange scene greeted her. The theater was being mobbed. People were spilling out onto the sidewalk, the box office area being too small to hold them, and more were coming to join them. Pedestrians were having difficulty walking by. A single policeman, sent, no doubt, by Inspector Kirk to intercept Mildred Trane when she arrived, was blowing his whistle without stop. He was soon joined by three more of the foot patrol, but the increase in their numbers could not stanch the flood besieging the box office for tickets. The evening's performance was sold out, as a placard a theater employee tried to place in front of the door indicated, but he was swamped by eager theatergoers. People on the street were waving their hands, resisting the police who, in vain, were trying to hold them back. Lily watched in amazement from the curb. Several people insisted on joining the line in front of the box office. Though there was no room, they pushed forward anyway. The police were overwhelmed. A few people were able to elude the police and enter the jammed area beyond the doors. One of them, in a plain cloth coat and a cloche hat, had a familiar walk. Lily hurried to the entrance doors to peer inside and was knocked aside by an avid theatergoer. The cloth coat and the cloche were gone. And suddenly, so were the agitated would-be patrons. It was five o'clock. The producer had found a way to have his star enter the theater undetected. Lily wondered how much the mob scene had cost him.

One policeman tipped his hat. "Good evening, Miss Chasen. I see your friend couldn't handle seeing the play again. You're very early, you know."

"I know Sergeant Reilly, but this was the quietest place I could think of to wait after a hectic day of work. It's a good play. Have you seen it?"

"No. Controversial would be the better word, so I hear. It's got a moral, at least."

"Ah, Sergeant, the 'at least' is the whole point of the play!"

"Been shopping, I see." He pointed to the milliner's bag. "I knew you modeled for her, but I didn't know you could afford one of her hats."

"I can't. This is on loan. Have you seen Uncle Harry today?"

"In the morning. I guess it's all right to let you in to rest. You do have a ticket?"

Lily held it up. Sergeant Reilly escorted her inside and tipped his hat again. Mildred Trane might have started dressing for Act 1, but Lily thought it wise not to wait. This might be her only chance to have a heart-to-heart with her husband before their worlds collapsed on them. Stagehands and actors smiled as she passed them in the hallways. No one spoke to her or stopped her. She had, as it were, become almost part of the fabric of performance nights. She knocked on a dressing room door. It was opened by the star herself.

"What is it?" came the anxious request.

"Your husband is not dead."

Mildred Trane staggered back, but Lily was quick in preventing a fall. "I don't know whose remains are sitting in your Victorian urn, but they are not Roland's. The salesgirl remembered well the man who bought the hat for Lavinia Lake, that is, after half his mustache fell off and his beard got caught on another Daché creation."

Mildred Trane could not help but laugh, but she continued laughing uncontrollably until Lily led her to a chair and clasped her hands. Tears were streaming down her face.

"If you still want him or want to see him or talk to him, he will probably be at the opening of a new burlesque show." Lily unfolded the advertisement she took from her purse. "He doesn't know Lavinia Lake is dead. He can't have been in love with a woman he's only known for two weeks. A dead Roland cannot be charged with the murder of Suzie Sweet or the attempted murder of Jimmy Carlton. Now he'll either face a jury or continue on the run. In either case, you are not likely to have a private meeting with him before Inspector Kirk creates chaos in your lives."

"The audience expects to see me. They'll be upset, and our producer will be upset, but it can't be helped. Back me up with Edgar Davis," she said as she headed to the door.

Chapter Twenty-Four

The patrons were in their seats, and there was a low hum of voices as Mildred and Lily entered to see the show, the show for them being Roland Trane in costume. After one look, the drama would begin, but the lines that would be spoken would be unrehearsed and from the heart, the soft part of the heart, hoped Lily. Declining an usher's assistance, they stood in the back of the burlesque theater looking at backs of heads, wondering which one was that of the deceased husband. A gentleman in a tuxedo walked to the center of the stage, and in a deep, resonant voice announced: "It is with great regret that, for reasons beyond her control, Lavinia Lake will not appear tonight. However, a very beautiful and accomplished young lady will delight and entertain you this evening. You'll be seeing more of this talented beauty in the future, the remarkable Miss Laura Young!" The tuxedo retreated, and someone in an aisle seat stood up. The mustache and the beard were in place, but it would have been clear to even a casual acquaintance that it was Roland Trane. Lily stepped to a side behind a row of seated spectators. The only one visible to the man as he walked to the rear was Mildred Trane. He stopped in front of her.

"Are you responsible for this?" His head tilted toward the stage.

"No, but I must talk to you about Lavinia and, if you wish, about us." Two ushers' chairs were up against a back wall. They took them and faced each other. "Lavinia is gone. She didn't deserve this, no one deserves this, but someone, some enemy—hers, yours, I have no idea who—has murdered her."

Roland Trane stared at his wife. "How? Where?" His voice cracked.

"The head of the burlesque company went to her room when she wasn't in her dressing room getting into costume for the show. She was on the floor with a knife in her back. He called the police, then checked with her home company in Philadelphia, who couldn't account for the loss of their star, but said she had been the recipient of your ashes and had mailed them to me, as you requested. Inspector Kirk, wandering our living room, waiting for my return, came across your ashes in an urn. He tested them and discovered they were human remains."

Roland nodded. "A neighbor gave them to me. They were his uncle's. He hated the man and was glad to get them off his mantel without actually tossing them himself."

"I kill my husband in Act I of our play, and I gave the inspector your letter to prove that I had not done the same in real life. I'm sorry about Lavinia, truly I am. Every life is precious. I was devastated when you came back to me as you did." Mildred looked down, thinking of nothing more she could say to her husband.

Roland spoke as in a dream. "She had a sad past, no upbringing to speak of. The only appreciation she got was from the wrong people, people who taught her to steal, to cheat, to become expert at forgery. I thought I could help her. She wanted to be helped. She didn't know who I was, didn't care. I offered her a hand, and she took it. It was only two weeks, but it seemed much longer, and now she's gone. Probably by the hand of someone who didn't want her to find a way out of her miserable life. I tried to help her, and I hurt her instead, murdered her really, as if I'd used the knife myself."

"It's wrong to think that way, Roland. You tried to make something out of her life and yours. No one will fault you for that. You mustn't fault yourself."

"I couldn't make our marriage work, and I couldn't make friendship with this poor, young thing work. Why is that, I wonder? Why can't I make my life work for me?"

"You can. We can, if you want us to try together. If there's a role you want to play, you can. You are very convincing in *The Ladder*."

"You want me to live in a land of make-believe all my life?"

"No, I want you to live your dreams; surely you have more than one, and after you've tried and enjoyed them all, keep the ones that work best for you, that give you feelings of satisfaction the others do not. Wearing your dreams will make you a pretty exciting fellow. I've a mind to try on some of my own, too. I love to act, but there's more I'd like to do."

"We'll seem pretty silly walking around in dreamland."

"Not to those who mean the most to us. Not to your sister or your mother, not to Willie or Jimmy. They'll be happy for us."

"Shouldn't you be performing tonight?"

"Yes, but it doesn't matter."

"It will matter to your fans. I've read the newspaper reports. I have to get you over there."

Mildred looked at her watch. "We'll be just in time for Act IV, modern times, the times we're trying to grapple with ourselves. You'll play your part, too. Let's go!"

Lily stepped out of the shadowed corner. "That's unrealistic, Roland. Your ashes saved you from arrest for the murder of Suzie Sweet and for the attempted murder of Jimmy Carlton with William Branten's car. And by the way, your wife did not have an affair with Jimmy Carlton during your marriage."

Roland's eyes lit up. He was quiet for a moment. "Acting was one of my dreams, and I'm obliged to see it through in this play. I can't deny the inspector his dream of capturing, arresting and trying me for something I did not do, and he can't deny me mine."

They left the burlesque house and waved frantically for a taxicab. "Or maybe," pondered Roland as they entered the vehicle, "maybe I can deny him his dream. Mine has at least a six-month run."

"More," exclaimed Mildred. "Theatergoers are practically breaking down the doors of the theater, mainly for the wrong reasons."

"Their reasons are their problem," asserted Lily. "You hold onto your dreams."

There were no policemen at the front or stage entrance to the theater. The play still had an hour more to run. Lily stood behind the last orchestra row in the packed theater. The director made no announcement of any kind before Act IV commenced. When Roland walked onstage, the audience roared its approval. When Mildred did the same, the applause was deafening. The characters froze in their roles until the acclaim subsided, though it seemed to take forever. The way the stars spoke their lines was a reviewer's dream, but this play was not constructed to please reviewers. It was devised to enter the hearts and souls of the audience, and this night, it surely did. *The Ladder* ended to wild applause, which turned thunderous when the stars of stage and front-page headlines appeared to take their bows, as in the wings, Inspector Kirk looked on.

*　　*　　*

The guests were assembled in the Morning Room for breakfast, but more important, to present ideas on what to do now. Roland had been arrested for the murder of Suzie Sweet and the attempted murder of Jimmy Carlton but would be released on bail that very day. Where would he go and what would he do before the trial took place? Mildred did not want her husband hounded by newspapermen. How could this be avoided? The people she had asked to consider this were friends: Robert Blair, engineer; Willie Simpson, historic building expert and writer; William Branten, Trane & Company's business and family attorney; Vivian Trane, sister; Eizabeth Trane, mother; producer Edgar Davis; director Murdock Pemberton; and two young women who had proven their loyalty, Lily Ann Chasen and Tenisha Jones.

"I expect the trial to commence within a month," said Branten.

"He might be better off in jail," said the engineer. "The press can't touch him there."

"We are not amused," said the producer.

"I'm serious, but if not, his best chance of going unnoticed is in my house. No one would think of looking for him there. He'd have the run of the place during the day when I'm out, as long as he is careful in the library, where I've set up a huge scale model of my next project."

"He'd be alone all day. How depressing," said Willie.

"Well, jail was my first suggestion."

"Roland can stay with me," volunteered Willie. "Even if the press knew he was there, they would leave him alone. I was once pestered by a newspaperman who wanted all the dirt on a distinguished family whose house I was going to feature in a book. I sent an architectural rendering of his open mouth—teeth, tongue, lips—to every other newspaper in town. Do you remember that, five years ago? It got rid of the pest and every would-be pest and was excellent publicity for the book. And I'm a witty chap. I'd take his mind off the fix he's in."

The matriarch spoke. "Didn't you propose to Mildred in the past? My son might not appreciate your current friendly overtures, which would keep him away from Mildred."

"Yes, we don't want to keep a couple apart, especially now that a reconciliation has begun. It has begun, hasn't it?" Vivian looked at Mildred, who did not respond.

"Roland could stay with our family," said William Branten. "As his attorney, that would be appropriate."

"Sounds exciting," said Willie wryly.

"I expect Roland to resume performing in *The Ladder*. That will keep everyone but the audience away for a good part of the day, and Mildred can see him daily. I can set up sleeping accommodations for him in the theater, if the strain outside becomes too much for him. What do you say, Mildred?"

"Well, Edgar, I'm seeking advice to determine if there is anything that will make life more comfortable for Roland than what I would prefer, which is keeping him at home with me until we head for the theater."

"May I suggest that finding the murderer before the case goes to trial would serve Roland best?" All eyes turned to Lily.

"That's right!" exclaimed Willie. "Who had the best motive for murdering Suzie Sweet and trying to murder Jimmy Carlton?"

"Roland. That's why the police arrested him." The engineer got looks that could only be called nasty.

"How about you, Branten?" Willie pursued. "Why did you lend Roland your car, and don't repeat what you told the police, that his was in the repair shop, because he could have rented one. Did you want him to kill Carlton because he had an affair with Mildred ages ago and you wanted Roland out of the way so Mildred could be free to find a husband more worthy of her, even though she didn't want a husband more worthy of her, you prig?"

"Now just a minute, you insolent excuse for a man! You no doubt think that you were worthy. Mildred saw through that thin veneer of a heart you possess. Don't you dare impugn my motives and my integrity!"

"Gentlemen, please. This is not helpful at all." Mildred Trane stepped between the men in case the verbal barrage escalated to something more.

Lily spoke again. "Mildred and Roland are important to each of you, so it is not unreasonable to posit the theory that one of you is a murderer. Is each of you willing to explain why you could not be?" There was a moment's uneasy silence.

"I say, that's a rather cheeky proposition," said Willie Simpson, "but I'm willing to start. Not once in the last ten years have I taken the offensive against Roland and proposed marriage to Mildred. If she was willing to put up with his adolescent behavior and gross affairs, then I was willing to put up with them. Her happiness was important to me. If she thought marriage to me would make her happy, she would have married me before she met Roland. I'm content that I tried to give her my name. Some women are givers, not takers. They must give their hearts, their help, their love, their undying loyalty, no matter what, to those in need. Roland was in need, great need. He couldn't seem to succeed in anything he turned his hand to, including marriage. I honor Mildred for that. I would not want the man dead who made her happy. Anyway, I was still in my office when William Branten's car targeted Mr. Carlton."

"I don't like the way you phrased that, you ignorant twit." Branton was livid. "I've seen you lolling and laughing and generally making a fool of yourself at social functions, and I've read your books. Rather snide and snotty, aren't you, about the people whose homes you pretend to revere? I reported my car stolen after Roland had done with it and returned it me, and it's insane to think I would want to destroy a client whose company provides 60% of my income and whose family I have loyally served for the last thirty years."

"There's not much for me to say," said Robert Blair. "I've never in my life been to a burlesque show, I don't know how to use a gun, and I can't drive a car. I take public transportation. It's reliable, safe, and less costly. I do on occasion take a taxicab," he relented.

"Well, you can hardly think that I would want to interfere in my son's life," said Elizabeth Trane. If I had, I would have done it long ago. I've been living quietly in France to shield Vivian and myself from it. I'm kept informed, of course. He is my son, and I make occasional telephone calls when my angst gets too great, but I believe children should live their own lives. One does what one can for them before they venture into the world, and one gives advice, wanted or not as situations demand, but each human being is responsible for his or her own life, and sets his own course, and I've allowed Roland to do that."

"You haven't allowed me to do that, Mother."

"I'm allowing that now. Your nurturing days are over. I'm here for you when you need me, as I've been for Roland. He has seen fit not to need me, but that doesn't stop me from loving him and wanting the best for him always. Suzie Sweet was a mistake, the last of many, but my philosophy would not allow me to issue commands, which would have been ignored anyway, only suggestions, vehemently expressed, to be sure, but only suggestions."

"You and your daughter arrived May 15, and Suzie Sweet was murdered May 16. You did have the opportunity to modify your philosophy and have her exit Roland's life," said Lily.

"The opportunity, yes, Miss Chasen, but not the will."

"Who kept you informed of Roland's activities, Mrs. Trane?"

"I called my son monthly. I asked questions, and he was honest with me."

"Your knowledge of his life came solely from those calls?" pursued Lily.

The matriarch hesitated.

"It's all right, dear lady," said Branten. "I informed Mrs. Trane of events concerning her son; I felt she should know. The rights of motherhood should not be denied a loving mother."

"Are you speaking as a philosopher or a lawyer, Mr. Branten?"

"Please, Miss Chasen! I appreciated the information."

"Do you drive, Mrs. Trane?" asked Tenisha.

"Yes, I do, Miss Jones, but I did not borrow William's car after Roland used it, and I have no knowledge of this Jimmy Carlton. He was in my daughter-in-law's personal life before Roland, and he's only been in her professional life for the purpose of play reviews since then. My daughter-in-law has strict moral principles. She is not a married woman who has affairs on the side. She's the best thing that has happened to Roland since I allowed him to make his own way in life. I want the murderer found because I believe every life has value, and I want justice for the dead and to my son, who is being falsely accused, I'm sure to the great joy of the actual murderer. The police are so illogical. Do they think Roland would attend the performance of a woman he had just murdered? He was as shocked and revolted at this senseless murder as Vivian and I were."

"Miss Trane, did your mother keep you informed of your brother's behavior?" asked Lily.

"Somewhat, and I could read between the lines. I had to, to comfort Mother, but I did not renew my acquaintance with the land of my birth by committing murder, although I can drive a car, and I know how to use a gun. Roland showed me for my protection, and I know he hid it in a box in his clothing closet."

"So there! Is that it, Vivian?" asked Lily.

"Well, you should believe me," pouted Vivian Trane.

"Don't look at me that way, ladies. I certainly don't involve myself in the lives of my scriptwriters and cast. I have enough to contend with without that." Producer Edgar Davis folded his hands.

"Mr. Pemberton, the police are unable to account for that steel box crashing to the stage just inches from Mildred Trane. How do you account for it?"

"If I could account for it, Miss Chasen, I would have told the police."

"After penning eighteen versions of *The Ladder*, Mr. Pemberton, it was generous of you to agree to direct a nineteenth version written by someone else. If the latest version were a success, it would put your eighteen attempts in the shade. As you made directing decisions, did you have this in mind?"

"You've seen the results of my decisions on the stage, Miss Chasen. Did they in any way undermine the effectiveness of the story or the message? I've always wanted *The Ladder* to succeed. As for being in the shade, I'm used to it. I get a private appreciation of my work, and that's enough, or at least it will do. I've never been able to shake the world, what of it, but I'm no murderer."

"Mildred Trane, if we're considering possible murderers, we can't exclude anyone."

"I don't ask to be excluded, Lily, but obviously, I could not have been above the stage attempting to kill myself and on the stage performing at the same time. As for Roland's affairs, had I wanted to kill his women, I had the opportunity to do it for ten years. Actually, I'd gotten used to expecting them. It's comforting to know what to expect. There were no big surprises in my private life, and certainly I would never have aimed an automobile at my loyal supporter Jimmy Carlton. Well," she said, rising from her chair, "I haven't heard any suggestion better than the one I proposed for Roland when he is released on bail today. We'll be together, at least, and see what tomorrow brings."

Tomorrow brought an invitation.

Chapter Twenty-Five

"We're going to Newport!" Bernard Singer was euphoric. "Alice Vanderbilt wants to open the summer season at The Breakers with a fashion show as well as a ball, and we will have the privilege of obliging! We have Mildred Trane to thank for this. She wanted Roland out of New York City for the summer, and Mrs. Vanderbilt invited them to stay at the mansion. She has accommodations for me and six models in town for a week before the event. She's hired a ten-piece band, and you girls will be descending the massive staircase in the Great Hall as they play. Lee, I want you to work with them to decide on music suitable to the clothes we'll be presenting. Make sure you have no other modeling appointments for the next three days; I'll need to confer with you about this. Sue will be disappointed that she won't be with us, but the piano they're moving from the music room for the occasion will be played by the bandleader. All the models will have to practice, practice, practice. Negotiating those steep stairs gracefully can be tricky, especially in evening gowns. I'm taking that into consideration as I design the show.

"Every article of clothing we're presenting will be new, and I'm adding a magnificent gown that has been floating through my brain since *The Ladder* re-opened. The model for that creation will be Mildred Trane! The gown will be modern, glamorous, gorgeous, wearable and inspired by the play. Think of it, summer at Newport—the opulent Breakers, the charm of the Gilded Age, the cream of society, women who appreciate style, magnificent balls and private parties, ocean waves breaking on the shore, the hectic calm—and Singer Couture in the middle of it all! What a treat, what an honor! It's about time!"

* * *

The week of rehearsals went quickly, and opening night at The Breakers began to unfold. It was five o'clock, and a delightful ocean breeze caressed the guests at Alice Vanderbilt's cocktail party. Strolling across carefully clipped grass, they paused to select canapés from waiters, chat with friends and acquaintances, and be introduced to people they had never met but who others thought they should meet. Returning from time to time to replenish their glasses with assorted libations at the banquet tables manned by a smiling staff, they got exercise as well as fresh air and the sight of distant yachts. Lily Chasen and Tenisha Jones observed with pleasure the relaxed, yet animated scene. They saw Jimmy Carlton, framed by rocks and ocean waves, in a group of familiar faces.

"Mr. Carlton, so good to see you. You're looking well."

"Ah, Miss Chasen, as long as automobiles are not allowed to ride on the grass, I am safe, bolstered by an edict from Mrs. Vanderbilt that no one attempt to run me down during her party and ruin the convivial nature of the event. I've never before covered a fashion show, but as a drama critic covering the foremost actress of our time, inadvertently I'll be covering all you model-ladies as well. Beware!"

"We'll do our best," said Lily, "but I think Mrs. Trane will outshine us all tonight." She grasped Mildred's hand and shook Roland's. "You have a darling friend in Mrs. Vanderbilt. I see the difference in you both already."

The Tranes smiled, and Roland inhaled deeply. "Much better than the air in jail." He was interrupted by several newcomers, who effusively greeted him, and Lily and Tenisha stepped away, accepted offered canapés and wandered toward a lightly occupied area of the great lawn.

"It's a pity, Ten. William Branten will no doubt successfully defend Roland. The evidence against him is filled with holes. To kill instead of banish Suzie Sweet because she upset him is ludicrous.

He's had and dropped many women before her. And to clear out your clothing closet and leave your gun in clear view on the floor casts more suspicion on an unknown murderer who placed it there than on the revolver's owner, whose fingerprints would, of course, still be on it after a gloved assailant had dispatched Miss Sweet. The jury that will see Roland Trane as a philanderer is hardly likely to see him as a moron. He arrived an hour early for a front row seat at the theater to see Lavinia Lake perform, spoke to his neighbor who likewise came early, and was in his seat when Miss Lake was murdered. His neighbor, whose name the police have, will vouch for that. Yes, Roland Trane will soon be free of the law's tentacles. William Branten and the lack of evidence will see to that. But the murderer will not be caught. There's not a shred of evidence linking anyone else to the two murders or to the attempted murders of Mildred Trane and Jimmy Carlton. And that's a pity."

"All the more so," said Tenisha, "because we know who the murderer is, but we cannot create evidence that does not exist."

Lily looked at her friend with wonder, and her eyes grew big. "Yes, we can! There is a tale the murderer will believe, but it will put a good man in harm's way. He's already had one escape from death. He may not wish to tempt fate with another."

"Jimmy Carlton. He just might. We lose nothing by asking. What do you have mind?"

The women walked and spoke, and only stopped when the sound of the waves began to impede on their conversation. They found themselves farther from the party than they had expected, and hurried back to find Carlton and propose their scheme. It was five-thirty. Jimmy Carlton, who had just been handed a cocktail, was looking thoughtful. The models asked him to join them for yet another stroll.

"Are you thinking about justice, Mr. Carlton, and whether Roland will get it?" asked Lily. "He will. Are you wondering whether you will get it, whether your assailant will be found? You know it was not Roland." Carlton nodded to Lily. "He will not be found without your help, but you will be exposing yourself to danger. You may not want to place yourself in that again."

"Do you know who this person is, Miss Chasen?"

"We're pretty sure. If you tell this individual a convincing lie, he will reveal himself. No evidence exists that can do it."

"He tried to kill Mildred, too?"

"Yes."

"Might he try again?"

"Probably not."

"Probably not? You say probably!"

"Probably not, but there are no assurances," said Lily.

"I suppose you know how I feel about Mildred, how I've always felt."

"We know. Would you like to hear our proposition?"

"Yes, Miss Chasen."

"There is a cement-block floor outside the room in the boarding house in which Lavinia Lake was staying. Some wet cement was roped off in a corner. There was none near Miss Lake's doorway, but you will assert that there was. It was five o'clock. Roland, arriving early for a good seat in the theater, was in it when the murderer entered her room. You, seeking something sensational for your column in *Variety* and taken with the advertisement for *Stitched Time*, and particularly with the accolades heaped in it on Miss Lake, decided to speak to her briefly before the show and at greater length after its conclusion. The manager of the boarding house was unable to dissuade you from seeing her, but fearing your arrogant attitude, he directed you to a second-floor room, the one above Miss Lake's. After you were informed of your mistake by an angry towel-clad young lady at the door, you began to descend the stairs, and saw a man emerge from the room the damp lady above had told you was Miss Lake's. You saw him hurry down the stairs. As you approached Miss Lake's door, you saw a man's shoe print in the cement by the stairs adjoining her room. Seeing blood trickling from under her door and fearing the shoe print belonged to Roland Trane, you loosened the cement block, covered it with the newspaper you were carrying, and hurried away yourself. It was more important for you to spare Mildred Trane than to see justice done to a woman who was Roland's latest adventure in adultery, so you did not reveal your acquisition of the murderer's shoe print. At home, you measured the shoe print and obtained Roland's shoe size from Mildred. You then realized that the murderer was not Roland. This evidence, in addition to the verbal testimony of Roland's theater neighbor, would be powerful affirmation that Roland Trane did not murder his latest female acquaintance. You want his attorney to have this evidence, which will put the final nail in the coffin of accusations against Roland."

"I'm mesmerized by that story!" exclaimed Jimmy Carlton. "If I didn't know you'd made it up, I'd believe it myself, Miss Chasen! But won't the murderer wonder why I'm offering the shoe print to him and not attorney William Branten? Do you expect him to believe that I would accept a bribe for the shoe print and my silence?"

"No," said Tenisha. "We want you to offer the shoe print to William Branten."

"But I don't understand. Who is the murderer?"

"William Branten."

Chapter Twenty-Six

The Music Room was in its element. It had people, lots of people, who had come to hear music of the past amid a carved and painted antiquity on walls and ceilings and the warm glow of the massive chandeliers overhead. Most sat on folding wooden chairs, but a lucky few sat on the red brocaded chairs near the dormant fireplace across from the piano and strings that would perform the program's offerings. Dressed in period costumes, the players assembled to play brief masterpieces by Baroque charmers William Boyce and C.P.E. Bach, followed by a Mozart concerto. The set was completed by a Tartini piece that no ordinary violinist could play, but the result must have been very close to what the great composer/violinist himself had achieved in his time, so long and appreciative was the applause for the performer. No face betrayed anxiety about anything, but this was a society gathering. After Lily and Tenisha explained to Jimmy Carlton where he and Branten were to meet and what Carlton was to say, they watched him go off to speak to the attorney. Before they joined the cocktail crowd en route to the Music Room for the evening's concert, Lily had used the house telephone to call the police, who would, she was told, be in the adjoining rooms on either side of the bedroom in which Carlton would face Branten for what was to be the conclusion of the murder case, if all went well. As the music played, both Lily and Tenisha mused on the loyalty and daring of a good friend. They shuddered that he might be giving his life for someone he highly prized. They knew it wasn't Roland Trane. There would be a policeman on either side of the door in the hall as well, but it was deemed risky to have one under the bed or scrunched in a closet where he could be detected by Branten, who might choose to examine the room before speaking to Carlton. Even now, while the music played, the police were assuming their posts. The Tartini and the applause ended, and the guests slowly made their way to dinner under the stars.

A dozen round tables and Chinese cane chairs awaited the diners. There was a full moon, but its light was augmented by candles on the tables. The violinist who had awed them all with the Tartini was strolling the area playing Johann Strauss. The lively music that energized the nightclubs and the musical stage would come later, at the ball following the fashion show. It was almost seven o'clock. The first floor of the mansion would be rife with preparations for the rest of the evening, which would take place in the Great Hall. Upstairs, the rooms would be empty. The Vanderbilts were with their guests. Tenisha had dashed up to make sure of this while Lily kept an eye on the two protagonists. The policemen were in place and well-armed. The young model returned at seven, in time to see Jimmy Carlton and William Branten make what looked like apologies to neighbors at their respective tables as they departed. Lily and Tenisha looked blankly at their tablemates, who were attempting to engage them in conversation. They could not speak or eat a bite. The other women made light of the dieting females, but the men—Willie Simpson, Robert Blair and Roland—were concerned. At 7:10 the models rose, able to bear the suspense no longer.

"I hate to take the men away, ladies," said Lily, "but think about what you can speak of in their absence! Robert, Willie, Roland, will you come with us?" They would, and they did.

As they entered the Great Hall, shots rang out from the floor above. Suddenly, a man vaulted down the stairs to shouts of "Stop him!" from a uniformed policeman. The three men below rushed to do so as the runner reached the bottom of the stairs. He pushed Roland to the floor, sent the engineer sliding twenty feet across the Great Hall, and punched Willie into one of the chairs being set up for the fashion show. As the man turned to make a running exit through the Great Hall's doors, Lily stuck out her foot, and William

Branten went sprawling. Seconds later, the police were at his side. He was unconscious.

"Why, it's Branten!" exclaimed Roland Trane.

"'It' is correct, Mr. Trane," said Lily. "No human being could cold bloodedly murder two people and attempt to murder two more."

A shaken Jimmy Carlton was slowly walking down the stairs, never releasing his hold on the thick iron banister. "He tried to knife me! What schemes you dream up, Lily!" As he reached the bottom of the staircase, he nearly slumped to the floor, but the men caught him, held him up and edged him toward a chair.

"Dan, is the ambulance on the way?" asked the police chief. He was assured that it was. Now everyone was seated— the police chief waiting for the ambulance and the Trane party waiting for an explanation.

"Branten needed money, lots of it," said Lily. "After thirty years, he was very familiar with your home, Roland. A new bride with a new prenuptial agreement was essential to him. You would pay dearly for it. But Mildred wouldn't leave. He came in through the servants' entrance and tried to push Mildred down the stairs, but your cry for help diverted him. Soon he was at the front door, feigning concern at your wife's belief that she had almost been pushed to her death. You, Roland, should be careful with the library ladder. It isn't the first time you've kicked it out from under you. Branten accompanied you and Mildred often to the theater for rehearsals, and was acquainted enough with it to attempt to kill her with a falling steel box filled with Newport Beach rocks he'd collected in the days when he could afford an entire summer here. He tried to strangle Mildred, mistaking her maid, fantasy-dressed in her clothes, for her. He was successful in killing Suzie Sweet. He was afraid she might reveal that she had been his mistress before she became yours, and he couldn't take the chance that, despite his thirty years of service, you might discharge him. Sixty percent of his income came from the Trane business and the Trane family. Since Miss Sweet had been seen talking to a columnist reputed to engage in sensational journalism—sorry, Jimmy—he couldn't chance leaving him alive either. If *The Ladder* brought you and Mildred together, Branten was lost. The loan sharks were getting very hungry. And yet with you in the dock, not so lost. Income from a criminal trial would set him back on his feet."

"Lavinia Lake had to die," continued Tenisha, "because she had been catapulted at an early age into a life of crime, of late with extortionists and the very loan sharks to whom Branten owed a huge debt. If she revealed this to you, your opinion of him might plummet, followed by his income. It was all about money. Justice didn't matter, loyalties didn't matter, people didn't matter, except one—himself. Are you all right Jimmy?"

"Fine. Wow!" He shook his head to clear it.

Roland Trane put an arm around him. Saving the life of a man whose wife appeals to you has to go down in some sort of record book, so Roland's look seemed to say. Needing something to do, however trivial, the men started helping the staff set up the chairs for the fashion show. The stretcher and bearers arrived as William Branten regained consciousness. The look he gave Lily as he was lifted off the floor was pure venom. Just then, Mrs. Trane entered the hall and saw her attorney.

"Is Branten hurt? Will he be all right?" she asked anxiously.

"No," replied Lily, "but everyone he tried to murder will be from now on."

"But why, why?" exclaimed the astonished actress.

"Expensive living, expensive mistresses, and loan sharks at the door. Pre-nups, murder trials, he had to keep them coming. Nothing personal when he tried to slam you with a steel box. It was all about money. Come on, we have to dress. We have a fashion show in half an hour!"

The fashion show was a smashing success, and Bernard Singer, watching from the last row in the audience, was beaming. When Mildred Trane appeared at the top of the stairs, turned slowly right and left and then around to reveal her ruffled backless dress, when she descended, gloved hand daintily on the railing, her long train trailing down half the stairs, with an elegance borne of years of assuming similar roles, her performance was wildly applauded. As she reached the bottom of the marble staircase, she segued into the arms of her husband, and the orchestra began playing Cole Porter. She reached behind, looped the train over one arm, and danced away, the signal for all the guests to join them on the marble dance floor. Lily breathed the first real sigh of relief she had allowed herself all day. The engineer danced off with Tenisha, and Mildred, still in Roland's arms, leaned over to say a few words to Lily as she danced by her.

An approaching Willie asked eagerly, "What did she say? Did she promise to buy Singer clothes forever? Did she promise you a part in her next play?"

Lily laughed. "She said, 'Thank you.'"

"Well, I should say so!" And Willie put his arm around her waist and danced her off, with both energy and grace, around The Breakers' Great Hall.

THE END